Slowly, he pushed aside her dressing gown

Then his eyes clouded over. "Wendy, when you said you were inexperienced, did you mean totally or comparatively?"

"What difference does it make?"

She felt his body stiffen. "It makes a lot of difference to me," Burke said in a grim voice. "I have no desire to deflower any virgins." Then his eyes softened, and he smiled regretfully as he closed the edges of the dressing gown and tied the belt securely, deliberately. "That's too great a gift to give someone like me." He shook his head, smiling.

Wendy understood at once. To a man like Burke, such an act would imply some sense of responsibility — require some level of commitment. He obviously didn't want that...not even on a temporary basis.

Books by Rosemary Hammond

These books may be available at your local bookseller.

Don't miss any of our special offers. Write to us at the following address for information on our newest releases.

Harlequin Reader Service
P.O. Box 52040, Phoenix, AZ 85072-2040
Canadian address: P.O. Box 2800, Postal Station A,
5170 Yonge St., Willowdale, Ont. M2N 6J3

The Scent of Hibiscus

Rosemary Hammond

Harlequin Books

TORONTO • NEW YORK • LONDON
AMSTERDAM • PARIS • SYDNEY • HAMBURG
STOCKHOLM • ATHENS • TOKYO • MILAN

Original hardcover edition published in 1984
by Mills & Boon Limited

ISBN 0-373-02674-9

Harlequin Romance first edition February 1985

CHAPTER ONE

THE small twin-engine plane began its slow descent towards the emerald dot of land in the midst of the blue sea. The bright tropical sunshine heightened the intensity of the colours that abounded on all sides—blazing blue sky, pale turquoise water, lustrous green foliage, brilliant red and yellow and purple flowers. The sensual beauty of the scene, however, was lost on at least one passenger, who sat by a window gazing listlessly down with unseeing eyes as the plane approached the Nassau airport.

She was thin—too thin—the fine bone structure of her face prominent under the taut smooth skin. The long black hair, still glossy and full of life, was drawn loosely back into a careless knot at the nape of her neck. The navy blue cotton jacket hung on her, at least a size too large, the dull colour emphasising the sallow skin tone which once had bloomed.

Even though she was unaware of it, the former loveliness was still perceptible, with a grace of movement and gesture that belied her depressed state of mind.

The announcement came to fasten seat-belts, but the girl by the window ignored the command. She continued to stare down at the approaching runway, oblivious to her surroundings, deep in a world of her own. The pert stewardess, frowning with disapproval, approached her seat.

'Miss Fuller,' she said, after consulting the passenger list, 'please fasten your seat-belt. We're coming in for landing.'

Wendy gazed up at her with blank eyes, still beautiful in spite of the hurt in them, a bright clear blue. She seemed confused. The stewardess pointed towards the two ends of the belt at either side of the seat, and Wendy finally seemed to grasp what was expected of her.

'Sorry,' she said curtly, with no other apology or explanation. Obediently, she fastened the belt and turned her head away. Tears were threatening again, and her pride would not allow them to be seen, even by a stranger.

She jumped a little as her seat-mate cleared her throat and touched her lightly on the arm.

'Are you okay?' the small redhead asked.

Wendy nodded and forced out a smile. 'Sure,' she said. Then, to be polite, she asked, 'Have you ever been to the Bahamas before?'

'I've never been *anywhere* before,' the girl exclaimed on a note of protest. 'My husband—my ex-husband, that is—had a very exciting social life, but I wasn't included in the more interesting parts.'

Wendy had to smile. The girl's tone was ironic, but without a trace of self-pity. She felt her spirits lift. 'Where are you staying?' she asked.

'At the Emerald Beach. How about you?'

'Same. I can just barely afford it, however.'

'I can't afford anything,' the girl replied tartly. 'I'm going to be working there.'

'Really? How exciting. Doing what?'

'Shorthand and typing for the guests. All the big hotels have these facilities. A friend of mine knows the manager, and when their regular girl quit, she called me and asked me if I wanted the job—and here I am. By the way, my name is Meg Burrows.'

'Wendy Fuller.'

'Well, it's nice to know someone here, although I don't imagine we'll be seeing much of each other. I understand the guests and hired help aren't encouraged to fraternise.'

Wendy was disappointed. It had been pleasant talking to the small redhead. Wendy was impressed with her courage in starting a new life and her lack of bitterness over past disappointment.

'Surely you'll have days off,' she said hopefully.

'I intend to find out all about that first thing,' Meg said firmly.

The plane touched down smoothly on the tarmac of the runway and slid to a full stop. Wendy slowly unfastened the seat-belt and gathered together her purse, an untouched book she had brought to read, and a small white travelling case. She followed Meg down the aisle to the door of the plane, along with the other passengers.

Stepping out of the air-conditioning into the full glare of the afternoon sun was like walking into a furnace. Immediately, beads of perspiration broke out on Wendy's forehead. By the time they reached the low pink stucco Customs building, her navy and white polka dot dress clung damply to her shoulders.

She and Meg entered the building along with other wilting passengers, who all breathed a concerted sigh of relief as the cool air of the interior descended on them.

The two girls stood patiently in line waiting for

the baggage to arrive from the plane. Meg wiped her still dripping forehead with a handkerchief.

'I think we both must have been out of our minds to come to the Bahamas in June,' the girl remarked, making a face. 'I had no idea it would be this hot.'

'It's pretty bad,' Wendy agreed, 'but I'd always wanted to come here, and the rates are so much cheaper in the summer.'

She didn't add that at the time her only concern had been to get away as quickly as possible, or that she had blindly chosen the first remote place she could think of, far away from her home in Baltimore.

And it was true that she had always wanted to visit the Caribbean. Friends had told her what a romantic spot it was, and how low the rates were in the off-season. She had dreamed of spending her honeymoon there, with David.

David! Just the thought of him brought angry tears to her eyes again. For the thousandth time she told herself she should have known better. Even now, standing in line in a public place waiting to go through Customs, with people milling all around her, she could feel the sudden, sickening wave of humiliation sweep over her.

To be twenty-five years old and still so gullible, so blind as to fall in love with a married man! But I didn't know he was married, she argued with herself once again. *That's no excuse*, her other self retaliated. *What did you expect? You knew that that singles' club was loaded with married men on the prowl.* But I didn't even want to go! *You went, though.*

She glanced at Meg, just ahead of her in line, and a pang of guilt hit her, sickening her. David could have been Meg's husband! The whole sordid affair made her feel so dirty.

The bored official glanced briefly through her two suitcases, asked a few curt questions, then stamped her entry permit and waved her on. Wendy moved in a daze towards the exit. She had to close her mind to the raging battle inside her head in order to function at all.

Out in front of the building several dilapidated buses waited for their passengers. Each one had a sign with the name of a different hotel stuck in its windscreen.

'There's the one for Emerald Beach,' Meg said, moving towards the row of buses. 'Come on.'

They settled themselves on the hard plastic seats, burning hot to the touch, and waited for their baggage to be stowed in the luggage compartment by the driver. The humid air in the hot bus was suffocating, and both girls began to perspire again.

All around them they could hear their fellow passengers chattering as they took their seats. There were obvious newly-weds among them, some retired couples, several single women of varying ages and a few unattached men.

They were both so uncomfortable with the heat that they didn't try to make conversation. Wendy was grateful for Meg's silence, and gazed out of the window deep in her own thoughts and memories.

'If only it didn't *hurt* so,' she had finally cried to Greta, her room-mate, in a rare moment of overt weakness. 'Why does it have to be so painful?'

Poor Greta had no easy answers for her and

remained silent, already burdened with guilt. She had coaxed and begged Wendy to go with her to the singles' club for weeks before Wendy finally gave in.

Wendy still, even during the worst of it, had sense enough to realise that time would heal her pain. It had only been a month since she had found out, a terrible month where she had struggled to keep going, to fulfil her normal everyday obligations, to appear calm and brave, to brush aside inquiries about David from her friends with a casual lie about an extended business trip.

Unable to force down more than a few bites of food at a time before her stomach rebelled, she began to lose weight. She hardly cared about her appearance any more.

'If only you'd talk about it,' Greta had pleaded. 'Cry! Have a tantrum! Throw something! But don't just hold it all in.'

Wendy had had to smile at that. But except for that one outburst, instantly regretted, she had remained silent. How could she explain to the ebullient, outgoing Greta? Greta, big and blonde, with nerves of steel and a calculating, casual attitude towards men. Easy come, easy go. You can't win them all. Here today, gone tomorrow. Those were Greta's mottoes.

Wendy was more reserved, with the intense fires of a passionate nature defensively banked inside her. For her, it had to be all or nothing. She couldn't help it. She had fervently wished she was more like Greta, but it wasn't in her.

The bus turned off the main road now into a curving driveway that wound around an immaculate lawn bordered by brightly coloured flowering shrubs.

'Home at last,' Meg said with a sigh of relief. 'Air-conditioning, here I come.'

At the entrance to the hotel, they got off the bus with the other passengers and made their way into the spacious lobby, cool and green, and dotted with potted palms. There was a view of the sea through the glassed-in rear of the room.

Meg turned to Wendy. 'Well, here's where we part company. I'm off to the salt mines.'

Wendy felt suddenly bereft at the thought of losing the company of the small redhead.

'We will get together, though, won't we?' she asked.

'Oh, sure,' Meg replied. 'I'd like to. I'll let you know when I have some time off and maybe we can go shopping or something.' She hesitated a moment, giving Wendy an appraising look. 'I know you've got something on your mind,' she went on in a gruff tone, 'and I won't pry. I just want to say that I've been through the mill myself, and if it will help, I've got broad shoulders.'

'I can see that,' Wendy said softly. She reached out a hand and touched Meg lightly on the arm. 'Thanks, Meg. I just might take you up on that.'

She watched as Meg went off down the hall to the employees' section of the hotel, grateful for her concern, but knowing the situation with David was one subject she was not likely to discuss with her.

Still, as she registered and made her way to her room on the second floor, Wendy felt more light-hearted than she had in weeks. Her room was a small one, all she could afford even at the reduced summer rates. It did face the sea, however. The hotel had advertised a sea view from every room, and it was for that reason she had chosen the Emerald Beach.

She glanced out of the small window now. The gleaming white sand of the beach stretched out beyond the hotel proper to the blue-green water of the Caribbean. To the right and curving around out of sight was a row of small cottages, independent units that, Wendy knew from the hotel's brochure, cost the earth.

There were clusters of palm trees, bright bushes of pink oleander, red poinciana, hibiscus and, along a wrought-iron stairway, a mass of scarlet bougainvillaea. Wendy felt a thrill of excitement at the lush tropical scene, so different from the crowded, noisy city she had left that morning. There were a few sunbathers dotting the wide stretch of sandy beach, the green and white striped hotel umbrellas raised to protect them from the glaring sun.

Wendy glanced at her watch and could hardly believe it was already six o'clock. She had promised Greta she'd call her as soon as she arrived. It was an hour earlier in Baltimore—maybe two. Then she realised it was Sunday and Greta would be home anyway.

She picked up the receiver and asked the operator to get the number for her. In a moment Greta's familiar hearty voice came on the line.

'It's me,' Wendy said. 'I'm here.'

'Oh, great,' Greta replied. 'I was afraid you'd change your mind halfway there.'

Wendy laughed. 'No, I made it all the way.'

'How is it?'

'Gorgeous.'

'Say,' Greta remarked, 'you sound different—almost human.'

Wendy laughed again. 'Has it been that bad?'

'Well, it hasn't been good,' Greta stated firmly. 'I've been worried about you, kiddo,' she added in a softer tone.

'I know, Greta. I'm sorry. I've behaved badly, childishly. It's hard to explain.'

'Don't even try. Just so long as you're okay. Let's both forget all about that rat.'

'Well, it's almost time to go down to dinner. The hotel is posh, the surroundings gorgeous, and I think I'm going to live.'

'Glad to hear it. Give me a call in a few days and let me know how things are going. How long do you suppose you'll stay?'

'As long as my money lasts,' Wendy replied firmly. 'I have no desire to hurry back to Baltimore.' Her voice softened. 'I still need a little time alone. Will you be okay in the apartment? I mean, the rent and all.'

'Sure. Not to worry. You paid your share for this month, and if it runs into July, I might take in a boarder.'

'Talk to you later, then. Bye.'

After she hung up, Wendy sat for several minutes, her hand still on the receiver, deep in thought. The conversation with Greta had revived memories that still caused her pain. She knew by now it did no good to fight them—they would come when they would come. But she now knew one thing she hadn't known before—they did pass, and that gave her hope.

The seating arrangements in the large dining room overlooking the beach were a mystery to Wendy. As she glanced around the room she saw that most of the tables were occupied by couples, and she decided that solitary guests must automatically be seated at a table for two. Apparently some official arbitrarily selected who would sit with whom, and that was that.

When the maître d' approached her and asked her name, she considered asking for a table alone. Before she could make up her mind, however, she found herself deftly guided to a table for two in the middle of the room.

She was glad to see that no one else was seated at the table. A tall, regal-looking waiter seated her and with an expert flick of one hand placed the spotless white linen napkin on her lap and with the other handed her a menu.

There was native calypso music in the background, a steel band playing softly, and gradually Wendy began to relax and enjoy herself. It was an enormous relief, she realised, to be among strangers, with no need to explain to anyone about David. She was convinced now she had done the right thing by taking leave from her job at the bank to come on this trip. She had no illusions that she was finally cured of mourning for David, but the change of scene was doing her a world of good and the moments of respite seemed to be coming more often and lasting longer.

Really hungry for the first time in a month, Wendy was so engrossed in the menu that she didn't notice that a man had been seated across the table from her. When she did, her nascent appetite threatened to vanish as her throat constricted. She gripped the large cardboard menu tightly. The last thing she wanted was to have to make polite conversation.

She glanced covertly across the table and saw that her dinner companion was staring at her oddly. He appeared tall, even sitting down, and was dark-haired and wearing horn-rimmed glasses. He had on a navy blue jacket of a crisp heavy linen material, a spotless white dress shirt and a muted tie.

Their eyes met briefly. Then, after a curt nod and a stern look of dismissal, he opened the book he carried, held it up in front of him and proceeded to read, stopping only to order his dinner.

Wendy was puzzled. She had never stayed in a resort hotel like this one before and wasn't sure of the protocol. She knew that in the dining room and lounge men were required to wear ties and jackets and no bathing-suits or shorts were allowed, but nowhere had she seen strictures against reading at meals. It seemed a little rude, she thought dubiously, but then it suited perfectly her own inclinations.

She decided that the next night she would bring a book of her own to read. Greta had thrust one at her at parting as a goodbye gift, but Wendy hadn't even glanced at it on the trip down.

She was halfway through the delicious meal of lobster thermidor, wild rice and a crisp green salad when she realised she was eating with gusto for the first time in a month.

Yes, she thought again, I was right to come. David seemed in another world, now, even another lifetime. Tentatively, she allowed an image of him to form in her mind once again, testing her reaction to the thoughts she had fought off so desperately for weeks. There was still a pang of longing for the smooth blond head, the candid blue eyes she never dreamed masked any deceit, the feel of his mouth on hers . . .

Her eyes clouded, and she knew it was too soon. To distract herself she took a sip of coffee and glanced across the table at her sequestered dinner partner. All she could see was the top of his dark head. Obviously a studious type, she thought, as she recalled the horn-rimmed glasses.

He held the book open in one hand and ate steadily with the other. The title of the book he was reading was *The Spirit of Medieval Philosophy*. Wendy wrinkled her nose. That was a little heavy for her tastes.

As if he could sense her gaze, he lowered the book so that she found herself staring into the iciest pair of grey eyes she had ever seen. Heavy dark eyebrows were constricted in a fierce scowl behind the glasses.

Quickly, Wendy lowered her eyes and nervously took a sip of scalding coffee, burning her mouth in the process. The book returned to its former position, and Wendy hastily gathered up her bag and left the table.

At first she was red with embarrassment over the incident. Then, as she threaded her way through the crowded room, she began to grow angry. He had made his point, she thought. She had no more desire to strike up an acquaintance with him than he with her. Certainly there was no excuse for such boorish behaviour, no matter what.

By the time she reached her room, her annoyance at the man had extended to men in general, their egotism, selfishness, callousness, and to her dismay she felt a wave of self-pity sweep over her as she recalled once again her shabby treatment at David's hands.

As she shut the door to her room behind her, tears were threatening and the gloom descending. 'No,' she said firmly to the empty room. 'I will not give in.'

I'm just tired, she thought. It was already past nine, and she had risen at five to catch the seven o'clock flight from Baltimore to Miami. She busied herself hanging up her clothes and putting things in dresser drawers. Then she took a shower and got into bed.

She picked up the book Greta had given her and glanced idly at the cover. It was very eye-catching, with a bright red background and the title in stark black lettering. It was entitled *This Bloody Land* and was a best-selling study of the causes and progress of the Vietnam war. The writer, a man named Flint, was a famous war correspondent, and Wendy knew that the book had already won several awards and was up for the Pulitzer Prize in journalism. Wendy's only brother, Steve, had been killed in that terrible war, and she read everything she could find on the subject.

She opened it at random and sampled a few phrases here and there. The man had a lively yet authoritative and serious style. It promised to be a good book, but Wendy's thoughts kept wandering and she couldn't seem to concentrate.

She turned out the light and tried to settle down, but thoughts of David kept appearing in her mind no matter how hard she fought them. David, with his sleek blond head and lazy grin, the guileless clear blue eyes that seemed so sincere and promised so much.

Yes, she thought bitterly, promises he never intended to deliver. She hated him now as much as she had loved him then, and she knew that she would not fully recover until those violent feelings turned to indifference.

Finally she dozed off in a fitful sleep, only to awaken to the darkness of a strange room. For a moment she couldn't imagine where she was. Then she remembered. She switched on the bedside lamp and glanced at her watch. Eleven-thirty. She sighed, wide awake now, in the peculiar state of exhaustion that was woolly-headed yet jumpy. She got out of bed and went over to the window.

There was a bright moon in the midnight-blue sky, bathing the tropical garden in a soft light. In the distance she could see its beams cutting a pale gold swarth through the sea, and she opened the window. It was still warm, but not as stifling as it had been earlier. Suddenly, on an impulse, she decided to go for a swim. The garden and beach looked deserted. She was a strong swimmer and in any event wouldn't venture out far, and she longed desperately for the refreshing, cleansing water.

She wondered if it was against the hotel rules for guests to go swimming alone at night with no lifeguard around, but she decided she was beyond worrying about rules. She just felt she had to get out of that room and into the sea.

Wendy found her string-coloured two-piece swimsuit, shed her nightgown and put it on. It was too large for her, too, but she was able to twist the straps of the bra to take up the slack. She was as full-breasted as ever, but had lost an inch or so around the back.

She tied a ribbon around her long dark hair, slipped on her white terrycloth beach robe and rubber-soled sandals and cautiously opened her door. It was deathly quiet in the corridor, and quite dim, with only two small lights burning at either end. Her room was on the second floor, and she crept down the stairs and slipped out the back entrance of the hotel.

She could hear music still coming from the lounge, soft and lilting, the marimba-like tones of the steel band instruments filling the air. It made her heart ache to think what could have been, if only David . . .

No, she told herself firmly. That's over. Forget it. Wendy ran lightly down the path to the beach and then across the soft sand past the curving row of small cottages until she came to the edge of the water. She looked around and decided to go to the left, where a small stand of date palms and a patch of oleander protected that portion of the beach from anyone who might be watching from the hotel.

She shed the robe and spread it out on the sand—it would serve later as a towel. Lightly she ran to the gently lapping surf and stepped into the water. It was pleasantly cool to the touch, and she lowered her body into it and began swimming lazily around, never venturing far.

It was heavenly out there alone under the moon and the stars with the palm trees towering overhead and the scent of hibiscus on the night air. The only sounds were the soft music drifting out from the hotel and the gentle tide breaking on the beach.

Wendy felt renewed in body and spirit after half an hour in the water, thoroughly relaxed and at peace. She was certain she would be able to sleep now. A heavy yet pleasant lethargy took possession of her, and she felt she could stay there just drifting forever.

Instead, she was jolted out of her idyll by a disturbance behind her, a heavy movement in the water. She turned to see a form about fifty feet away and heading straight towards her.

Her first startled thought was of sharks. Were there any in the area? She didn't know, and decided not to stay to find out. She stood up in waist-high water and began wading towards the shore as quickly as possible. It was only about twenty feet, but seemed a mile in the impeding water. Her heart began to pound as the sounds behind her came closer, and she deeply regretted her decision to come out here alone without checking with someone about sharks.

Finally, panting, she reached the shore. In her haste, she stumbled on a large outcropping of rock she hadn't seen in the dimness, and with a little cry of pain, fell forward on to the beach.

A shaft of fire shot up her leg. Wincing, she glanced down and by the light of the moon could see dark blood oozing down from a jagged wound on her knee. So penetrating was the pain that Wendy forgot all about her worry over the form in the water that had frightened her so.

Her back to the sea, she sat down on the sand and

gingerly stretched out her leg to examine the extent of her injury. She didn't even notice the man until he was squatting beside her, the water from his dripping body splashing on her.

Her knee stung so badly that she wasn't even startled when she heard him speak to her in a low voice.

'Are you badly hurt?' he asked. 'Here, let me take a look.'

'I don't think so,' she murmured. 'It just stings so.'

She felt a little giddy and leaned back, her hands flat on the sand behind her.

'It's the salt water that makes it sting,' she dimly heard him mutter. 'There's a spring nearby.'

He left her then, for a moment. She didn't budge. When he returned she saw that he was carrying something cupped in his hands. She could also see that he was quite tall, with broad shoulders tapering down to narrow hips encased in a dark pair of trunks. He had an unruly shock of black hair and came towards her with a purposeful, graceful stride.

She closed her eyes, then, steeling herself against further pain, but instead she felt a soothing sensation on her leg, wet and cool.

'Relax,' she heard him mutter. 'It's only fresh water to wash out the salt. Better put some antiseptic on it later, though. No sense risking infection.'

She opened her eyes and found herself gazing into the face of the man crouched beside her. The pale moonlight washed everything of colour, but she could see that the eyes that met hers were steely and brooding.

'Feel better?' he asked curtly.

'Yes, much,' she breathed. 'Thank you.'

His eyes narrowed still further, giving him a stern, forbidding look. A little knot of fear began to form at the pit of Wendy's stomach. Who was this man? She sensed danger in him.

'What the hell are you doing out here by yourself at night, anyway?' he growled.

He was so close to her, facing her, that she could hear his steady breathing, feel it on her face. Then she saw his gaze flicker down the length of her body, stretched out before him on the beach. The searching exploration of those veiled eyes made her feel naked in her scanty swimsuit.

His scolding tone, however, had banished the fear and made her angry.

'I might ask you the same thing,' she retorted sharply. 'What do you mean by sneaking up on people in the dark like that? You scared me half to death.'

'Feeling better, I see,' he remarked drily.

They glared at each other for a long moment. Suddenly Wendy became dimly aware that the warmth stealing through her was no longer primarily anger, but something else.

He was down on his haunches beside her, their bodies almost touching, their eyes locked together. She couldn't be sure in the dim moonlight, but she thought she saw his mouth quiver. They stayed that way in silence for what seemed like an eternity, until Wendy became acutely aware of the thudding of her own heart.

Something indefinable passed between them. Wendy had the odd sensation that they were suspended in space, alone in a magical world of sea and sand, moon and stars, and the heavy scent of hibiscus.

Suddenly he made an abrupt movement towards her. She shrank back instinctively, more afraid of the feelings surging up in her than she was of him.

He reached out a hand and put it gently on her cheek. 'You look very beautiful in the moonlight, you know,' he said in a husky voice. 'I thought for a moment there, when I first saw you in the water, that you were a mermaid.'

Once again his eyes travelled down the length of her body then back again to hold her gaze in his.

'Very beautiful,' he murmured.

Wendy could only stare at him, speechless, transfixed.

The next thing she knew she was in his arms, his mouth warm and soft on hers.

It felt so good to be held by a man again, to feel strong arms around her, the smooth skin of his body against hers, the roughness of his cheek, and she almost gave in to the impulse to flow with her feelings.

Almost, but not quite. Just as his mouth became more insistent and his hands moved from her shoulders to slide slowly down her bare back, she summoned all her power of will and pulled away from him.

'I—I'm sorry,' she said unevenly. 'My leg hurts. I must go.'

Without a word he drew away from her abruptly and got to his feet. He reached down a hand and helped her up. The spell was broken. It was as if the moment had never passed between them, their lips had never met. He even seemed grateful that she had stopped him.

'Will you be all right?' he asked, releasing her hand.

'Yes, of course. I'm fine now. Thank you for helping me.'

She turned and walked quickly off towards the hotel, picking up her robe on the way. She didn't dare look back until she rounded the curve of the beach and started up the path that led to the hotel.

He was gone. Wendy felt relief mingled with an odd prick of disappointment. He had let her go almost too willingly. She had expected a struggle, but the minute she had pulled away from him, he had released her.

There was something else, something she couldn't quite put her finger on, a little nagging question at the back of her mind, puzzling her as she made her way up to her room.

Somehow, the man on the beach had seemed vaguely familiar to her. Who was he? Did she know him? Had he been on the plane coming over from Miami?

She went into her room, locked the door behind her and leaned back against it, the feeling growing in her that she must have seen him somewhere before.

As she rinsed off the salt water under the shower she idly wondered if he reminded her of David. She didn't think so. David was so fair, and not so tall or muscular as the man on the beach who had towered over her and whose arms had felt so powerful when he had held her.

She smiled then, as she realised that the mystery

had so captured her attention and intrigued her that she had thought of David for the first time in a month with a degree of detachment.

And, she thought happily, as she dried herself and slipped on her nightgown, it was also the first time in a month that the old familiar sickening wave of despair at the mere thought of him was missing.

It wasn't until she had turned out her light and was drifting off to sleep that it suddenly dawned on her who the man on the beach reminded her of. It was her taciturn dinner companion!

She sat bolt upright in bed. Of course. There was no mistaking that dark head of thick hair, the heavy eyebrows, the brooding look, the flat planes of the cheekbones. Take off those horn-rimmed glasses and well-tailored suit and they were identical.

She lay back down again and began to wonder, to doubt her conclusion. It had been so dark on the beach, and in the dining room earlier she hadn't really had a good look at him, only a fleeting impression before he had buried himself behind that book.

Besides, she thought with a deep yawn, what difference does it make? The moonlight had got to both of them for a moment out there, but he was obviously no more interested in an involvement than she was.

She yawned again and in a moment was soundly, deeply asleep.

CHAPTER TWO

THE next morning Wendy was awakened by the ringing of the telephone on her bedside table. For a moment she felt disoriented, as one does in a strange bed, a strange room. Then she remembered. She reached for the telephone and muttered a sleepy 'Hello.'

'Hi, Wendy. It's me. Meg. Did I wake you up?'

'What time is it?' Wendy asked in a muffled tone.

'Eleven o'clock. Sorry if I woke you, but I only have one day before I start work full time, and yesterday you said you might want to do something. If you've made other plans, though . . .' Her voice trailed off weakly.

Wendy was instantly contrite. 'I'd love to do something with you today, Meg. Don't mind me. I'm always grumpy in the morning.'

'Are you sure?' Meg's voice was still hesitant.

'Positive. Let me get dressed and grab a quick bite in the coffee shop and I'll be raring to go. Why don't I meet you there in about fifteen minutes.'

'Sounds great. See you then.'

Wendy hung up and rolled back on to the pillows, stretching her arms high above her head. She felt oddly happy. It was wonderful to be here in Nassau, in this hotel; wonderful to be meeting Meg; wonderful, she realised at last, to be Wendy Fuller.

Testing herself again, she pictured David in her

26

mind and found that her heart didn't lurch, nor her pulses race. Could it really be over? She could even feel a little sad about that, as if forgetting diminished the quality of the affair.

Yet it hadn't really been an affair, she thought gratefully as she swung her legs over the side of the bed and slipped her feet into her sandals. She padded over to the window, drew the blinds and looked out at the sea. It was another perfectly clear day, with just a slight ripple on the water. There were only a few people out on the beach protected by the green and white striped umbrellas. It was probably blazing hot out there, she thought.

She went into the bathroom to wash and brush her teeth and noticed the swimsuit hanging on the shower curtain rod. She had forgotten last night's encounter on the beach. Now, remembering, she glanced down at her knee. The jagged gash had already begun to heal over. It was obviously only a superficial cut.

She stared at her reflection in the mirror. It hadn't been a dream. She raised her fingers to her lips where the stranger on the beach had kissed her. Yes, it had really happened.

But who was he? And if he was the same man who had sat across from her at dinner last night, so hostile and unfriendly, hidden behind that forbidding book, why had he suddenly turned amorous?

The moonlight, of course, she thought to herself, and smiled at her reflection. A light appeared in the blue eyes and she laughed. He had thought she was a mermaid. She had to admit that the mood of the romantic evening had worked on her imagination, too. Now, however, in the light of day, she was more sober, and, she realised, grateful she had broken away from him before the episode could pass beyond that one kiss.

It had been a pleasant interlude, she thought as she began to dress. She chose a cool dress of sea-green polished cotton from the cupboard and frowned a little as she noticed the way it hung on her. If her new-found appetite continued, she thought, that problem would soon be resolved.

She began to brush out her dark hair, then stopped, her arm suspended in mid-air. What in the world was she going to do about the man if he was indeed her dinner companion? She stood immobile, the brush still in her hand. She set the brush down and twisted her hair into a loose coil at the back of her head. There was no sense borrowing trouble. She'd see what his attitude was tonight. If he turned amorous she would simply have her table changed.

Meg was waiting for her at a table in the coffee shop, looking, Wendy thought, a little disconsolate. Her eyes lit up when she caught sight of Wendy, however, and she raised her hand in a little wave of greeting.

Wendy sat down. 'Am I on time?' she asked.

'On the dot. I hope I didn't wake you this morning. I'm a morning person myself.'

'That's wonderful,' Wendy said. 'I wish I were. It takes a cup of good strong coffee to get me moving in the morning. However, I'm usually bright-eyed and bushy-tailed around eleven o'clock at night.'

'Oh, not me. I konk out right after dinner.'

'It takes all kinds, doesn't it?'

The two girls smiled at each other.

The waitress appeared, a petite young girl, not more than sixteen, with a terminal case of the giggles. Wendy ordered a chicken salad sandwich and coffee. Meg had already ordered and was chewing thoughtfully on her sandwich.

'My husband was a night person,' she said. 'It's probably one reason why we didn't get along. Although we were making out all right until Baby Doll came along.'

'Baby Doll?' Wendy asked.

Meg waved a hand in the air. 'You know, his lady love, my successor in his heart, his paramour, mistress, whatever you want to call it.'

Her tone was light and mocking, but Wendy could sense the deep hurt underneath. How would it feel, she wondered, to give yourself to someone like that and have him betray your trust? Of course, that had happened with David, but at least it hadn't been a real commitment, nothing like a marriage or even a full-blown affair.

She felt Meg staring at her and found it difficult to meet her eyes. 'I—I'm sorry, Meg,' she faltered, 'that you've had such a bad time.'

'From the looks of it, kiddo,' Meg said softly, 'it hasn't been a picnic for you, either. Were you married?'

'No,' Wendy answered quickly.

'Was he?'

Wendy gasped. That was the one subject she wanted to stay off of. How would Meg feel if she found out her new friend had been some other husband's Baby Doll?

'Was he what?' she asked weakly.

'Married,' Meg replied.

Wendy didn't know what to say. What would Meg think of her if she found out her new friend had been involved with a married man? Besides, the hurt was still too raw for her to feel comfortable discussing it with anyone.

'I'm sorry, Meg,' she said finally. 'I really don't want to talk about it.'

'Sure,' Meg said quickly, lowering her eyes. 'I understand. I didn't mean to butt in.'

'It's not you, Meg,' Wendy continued. 'I mean, I want you to really understand.' Meg looked up then, and their eyes met. 'I came here to try to forget about it. There were too many reminders back in Baltimore. I don't want to talk about it or think about it. It's as though—oh, I don't know—as though I've had a terrible accident or illness, and the more I dwell on it, the harder it will be to get well. I want us to be friends, to have a good time together, not cry on each other's shoulders.'

Meg looked dubious for a moment, then her face brightened. 'Sure. I see. You're right. We'll forget all about the creeps. Onward and upward.' She raised her glass of milk in a mock salute. 'Here's to us.'

Wendy laughed out loud with relief. Meg seemed reassured. She lifted her own glass of milk, clinked it against Meg's, and they smiled conspiratorially at each other.

'I'll tell you what,' Wendy said as she finished up her sandwich. 'As soon as I feel really over the hump, I'll tell you all the gory details. We can compare notes, have a good laugh—or cry—and then forget all about it.'

'Good thinking,' Meg agreed.

It was barely a ten-minute ride from the hotel into the centre of the small city of Nassau. There were only two other passengers on the dilapidated bus; an elderly couple who made no attempt to speak to the two girls. The man dozed; the woman gazed stonily out of the window.

'Not many people going into town,' Wendy whispered to Meg after they had settled themselves by an open window.

'The rest of them have more sense,' Meg replied in a hiss.

Even though all the windows on the bus were open, it was stiflingly hot inside. The breeze was so humid and dusty that by the time they pulled up at the market square in the centre of town, both girls were panting and perspiring.

They got off the bus at the square and began to wander about the shaded open-air stalls of the market. There were colourful stalls of tropical fruit in wicker baskets—pineapple, apricots, papaya, mangoes, and several varieties Wendy had never seen before. Bananas hung in huge bunches from the rafters of the straw-covered ceiling, and there were cartons of dates and nuts set out on tables.

The two girls became so engrossed in the entrancing sights, sounds and smells of the busy market that they soon forgot their discomfort. There were stalls that sold brightly coloured scarves, others piled high with the beautiful basketwork the native women created, and others with raffia dolls and figurines.

The native people moved gracefully and spoke a

pleasant patois that had a melodic lilt to it, smiling and beckoning the tourists milling about to sample their wares. Wendy was impressed with their simplicity and dignity, their childlike naturalness, and lost herself as she wandered about.

There were children everywhere, beautiful little native boys and girls, naked except for colourful cotton shorts. Wendy saw one little boy, who could only have been two or three, hiding behind his mother's voluminous skirts and relieving himself in the dusty alley behind the stalls. She turned to Meg, hoping she had noticed. Meg raised her eyebrows and grinned.

They had barely begun to explore the market when the first return bus to the hotel appeared.

'I'm not ready to go back yet, are you?' Meg asked.

'Heavens, no,' Wendy replied. 'We're just getting started.'

They were standing in front of a stall that sold floppy straw hats. Meg was trying one on. 'How does this look on me?' she asked.

The hat was huge, and Meg's small face was lost under the wide brim. The crown was encircled by a ring of shiny raffia flowers in every shade of green. Wendy stood back, eyeing her friend.

'It is a little big,' she said at last. She began to search in the pile of hats for one a little more suitable for the petite redhead.

'I guess you're right,' Meg said wistfully. She looked at Wendy with a trace of envy in her eyes. 'I wish I were taller.' She took off the hat and handed it to Wendy. 'Here, you try it on.'

Wendy took the hat and placed it on her head.

Meg examined her critically. 'It looks great. You'd better buy it.'

'I don't know,' Wendy said hesitantly. 'I don't have much money to spend and I wanted to take back some gifts.'

'It really looks great on you,' Meg insisted.

'Oh, all right.' Wendy paid the smiling native woman. Her brightly coloured turban caught Wendy's eye. 'Meg, why don't you get a turban? If the native women wear them they must be effective against the heat.'

'No thanks,' Meg replied firmly. 'I'll settle for a smaller straw.'

They finally chose one that didn't dwarf the small girl's head and passed on.

'Let's take a walk through town,' Meg suggested. 'Maybe stop somewhere for a cool drink.'

They started off down the pavement of the main street and walked for an hour past the small shops. Catching sight of her reflection in a shop window as they strolled by, Wendy thought she looked quite jaunty in her sea-green cotton dress and wide-brimmed straw hat with the green flowers around the crown. She felt very happy.

At an intersection, Meg nudged her and pointed across the way to a large pink stucco building with the British Union Jack waving in the slight breeze of the sea. The building was surrounded by colourful gardens, eye-catching in the bright sunshine.

'That must be the Government House,' Meg said. 'Let's cross over and look through the gardens.'

They stood at the kerb watching the tall, regal-looking traffic policeman who stood in the centre of the intersection on a concrete pedestal. He was dressed in a spotless white tunic and helmet with dark trousers. As they watched, fascinated, he raised a white-gloved hand and blew his whistle to direct the traffic going their way.

Halfway across the street, Wendy glanced at the wide stairs leading down from the portico of the Government House and drew in her breath at the sight of the tall, slim figure coming down the steps towards them. it was her dinner companion, the man on the beach.

Quickly, she turned her head, grateful for the large straw hat that hid her from his view. She stopped and put a hand on Meg's arm.

'Meg,' she said, 'my feet are killing me. Let's go back to the hotel.'

Meg stared at her, blinking. 'Well, sure,' she said. 'We've probably had enough for one day, anyway. No sense overdoing it.'

They retraced their steps and walked back to the market square to wait for the next bus. They sat on the little stone bench at the bus stop, hot, sticky and tired.

Wendy began to feel foolish. Why had she turned and run from the sight of that man? He hadn't even glanced her way. Why had the mere sight of him unnerved her so? She pictured him again in her mind. He had been wearing light brown trousers and a well-tailored beige jacket. He was an impressive-looking man, tall, graceful, and with an air of confidence in the way he held himself, the way he walked. With an effort, Wendy dismissed him from her mind.

When the bus arrived they climbed into it wearily, grateful for even the small breeze that came through the open windows once they got moving. There were a few more passengers on the return trip, but except for complaining loudly about how uncomfortable they all were, there was little conversation.

Soon they pulled into the drive of the hotel, and Wendy turned to Meg. 'So you start work tomorrow?' she asked.

Meg made a face. 'I'm afraid so. It won't be so bad. At least the hotel is air-conditioned. And I have evenings free. We can't eat together, but maybe we could do something some night soon.'

They got off the bus and went inside. Wendy glanced at her watch—it was six o'clock, too late for a swim. The two girls said goodbye at the foot of the stairs, and Wendy watched as the small redhead walked off down the corridor to the employees' quarters, feeling suddenly lonely. She hoped they would see each other again soon.

In her room, Wendy stripped and straight away got under a lukewarm shower. It wasn't until she was drying herself, however, that she realised she would have to face that man at dinner that night. It was too late now to have her seat changed, and she didn't want to create a disturbance or call attention to herself. She promised herself she would make the necessary change first thing tomorrow morning.

Was it the same man as the one on the beach? She wondered about this as she hung up her towel. The thought disturbed her. She had pushed it out of her mind all day, but now, with a meeting imminent, she stopped to consider it. He had been so distant, almost rude, at dinner. His coldness had irked her a little, but she thought she preferred that to the desire she had seen in his eyes on the beach last night.

Standing naked in the middle of the room, Wendy put her fingers on her mouth, remembering the kiss. It had been such an odd experience, almost unreal—yet the kiss had been real enough. So had the feel of that hard strong body against hers, the masculine arms that had held her.

She laughed then, and shook herself a little, tossing back her loose black hair. None of that, my girl, she said to herself sternly. It was only the moonlight. Little more, really, than a dream.

She dressed quickly in a black sundress, a dress David had especially liked on her. She hadn't worn it in a month because of the memories attached to it. It had a low-cut bodice that was looser now that she had lost weight—it didn't hug her body the way it used to. The material was a silky cotton blend that flowed gracefully down from the waistline in a full pleated skirt.

As she smoothed the skirt down now, she couldn't suppress a pang of regret and longing or the tears that filled her eyes as she recalled how David used to put his hands around her small waist, his smouldering eyes fastened on the revealing bodice, the swelling of her breasts clearly visible above the low neckline.

Slowly, his hands would travel up her ribcage, always stopping just below the fullness. How she had longed for him to keep going. But some instinct had always made her stiffen before his hands actually moved over her breast. At the time she had regretted it, now she was glad that the affair, intense as it had been, had never progressed beyond passionate kisses.

She loved the dress. It always made her feel pretty, like a desirable woman. Still, it was too revealing to wear to dinner tonight, especially after last night on the beach, and Wendy felt shy about wearing it. There was no point in asking for trouble.

She had just about made up her mind to change into something more sedate when she spied her white crocheted shawl. It was a lovely wispy piece of woollen lace Greta had given her last Christmas. She slipped it over her shoulders and knotted it loosely in front of the low bodice of the black dress.

Surveying herself in the mirror, she decided that she looked quite modest now, even somewhat forbidding. On an impulse she picked up the book Greta had given her. Tit for tat, she thought defiantly. If he can read a book at dinner, so can I.

As she entered the dining room she gave her name to the maître d', who seated her at the same table she had occupied last night. Once again, she was the only one there. She enjoyed sitting there alone, listening to the music, the low hum of conversation, the clinking of glasses and silverware.

Perhaps he won't come tonight, she thought. In a way she hoped not. But in another, she couldn't help wanting to confirm her suspicions that he was, indeed, the man on the beach.

She ordered her dinner, and while she waited for it to arrive, she decided to start the book she had brought with her. As she read she became more and more engrossed in the story, a well-documented personal account of the war in Vietnam that was also lively, entertaining reading.

Deeply interested in anything about that dreadful war that had cost the life of her only brother, she hardly noticed when her dinner was served, and she continued to read while she ate.

Suddenly, her fork halfway from her plate to her mouth, she became aware of a dark shape looming over her from across the table. She looked up, startled, and found herself staring into those hooded grey eyes. He wasn't wearing the glasses tonight, and Wendy was immediately certain that he was the man on the beach.

She felt the colour rise in her cheeks, flushing her face. She opened her mouth to speak, but the look on his face stopped her. He was glaring at her, his eyes narrow, his lips curled in a look of contempt. She was so taken aback by the anger emanating from him that she gave a little gasp.

He made an angry gesture towards the book she still held in her hand, propped on the table in front of her plate.

'All right,' he said icily. He seemed to be holding a raging fury just barely in check with tremendous effort. 'What are you and what do you want?'

She could only stare at him, speechless with shock at the totally unexpected and irrational attack. What am I? she asked herself. How do you answer a question like that?

'Come on,' he was saying, his voice hard, his tone contemptuous, 'let's have it. Your little game is over. I repeat, what are you and what do you want?'

'What do you mean, what am I?' she asked in a bewildered tone.

'You know what I mean,' he snapped at her. 'Are you a reporter or just another groupie wanting to sleep with a celebrity?'

Wendy glanced furtively around. His voice carried so! She could see that the diners at the surrounding tables were gazing at them with undisguised interest.

'Look,' she said finally, her own temper beginning to rise, 'I don't know what you're talking about, but if you'll lower your voice and sit down, we can discuss it.'

This only seemed to infuriate him more. By now almost incoherent with rage, he pointed an accusing finger at the book she held.

'If you don't know what I'm talking about,' he said venomously through clenched teeth, 'how do you explain that book?'

'I don't have to explain anything to you,' she returned angrily. She *wished* he would lower his voice.

In an effort to comprehend what the maniac across from her was raving about, Wendy glanced down at the printed pages before her eyes. Then she shut the book and looked at the now familiar red and black cover. She could find nothing in either place to get excited about.

She turned the book over. There was a photograph, apparently of the author, on the back of the book. She felt a sudden rush of hot blood to her face as she instantly recognised it.

She glanced up at him—still glaring at her—then back to the photograph, then back to his face.

'You,' she stammered. 'You're Burke Flint. You wrote this book?' It came out sounding like a question.

'Very good,' he sneered. 'You're quite an actress.'

'Wait a minute,' she said slowly. 'Since I seem to be on some kind of witness stand, I'll admit to the crime of reading—*trying* to read—your book.' She gave him a nasty look. 'Is it that bad? I thought it was quite well-written myself.'

'Oh, come off it, Miss Whatever-your-name-is. Don't bat those big blue eyes at me.' He sat down abruptly.

'I wasn't batting anything,' she said, a cool edge creeping into her tone. 'I'm trying hard to keep from throwing your precious book at your head. It wasn't *that* good, you know. But you've aroused my curiosity. Just what is it that you find so criminal, so heinous, about my happening to be reading your book?'

'Happening!' he snorted. 'Try another one. I suppose you just "happened" to be seated at my table.'

Suddenly the light dawned. She stared at him, open-mouthed. 'You mean . . .' she spluttered. 'You think that I . . . Oh, no, nobody could be that egotistical. You can't mean you think I brought your stupid book here on purpose, had myself seated at your table on purpose!'

'Well?' he demanded. 'Didn't you?'

Wendy couldn't help it. In spite of her anger, she had to laugh. She shook her head. 'I don't believe it,' she said.

She could only stare at him. He was leaning back

in his chair, his arms folded across his chest, and his anger seemed to have dissipated.

'Oh, it's a familiar ploy,' he drawled. He leaned towards her, his elbows on the table. 'A good attention-getter for the poor unsuspecting writer. An attractive girl decides to entrap him, get him in bed, then use him. Is it money you're after? Or is it a story, an exclusive interview? Or just a thrill? I've found that fame is a potent aphrodisiac.'

Wendy had had enough. She was so angry now she could barely focus on him. 'Mr Flint,' she spat at him, 'you could be Robert Redford, Ernest Hemingway and the King of England all rolled into one, and I wouldn't want to get nearer to you than with a ten-foot pole.'

His lip curled in amusement. 'There is no King of England at the present time.'

'Oh, oh,' she spluttered. 'You're a dreadful, horrible, conceited man!'

She jumped to her feet and slammed the book down on the table. In the process a large tumbler of water began to jiggle precariously. Wendy reached out a hand to grab it, her white shawl coming undone and slipping to the floor in the process. But she was too late. The glass overturned and she gazed in horror, rooted to the spot, and watched the water slowly trickle over the side of the table into the lap of Burke Flint.

She raised her eyes to his, steeling herself for a renewed onslaught of indignation and outrage, but found instead that he was staring at her curiously, ignoring the water seeping into the legs of his trousers, an odd expression on his face.

'You're the girl on the beach,' he said at last.

Wendy coloured violently, suddenly aware of her naked shoulders and what the loose low-cut dress revealed to those probing eyes.

It flashed through her mind that she had been a fool not to have her table changed tonight, no matter how much trouble it would have caused. This arrogant, rude man made her uneasy.

Gathering herself together, she reached down to pick up her shawl, her heart still pounding. With a deliberate, unhurried gesture, she covered her shoulders with it and tied it firmly in place. Then, in as cold a voice as she could command, she said, 'You must be mistaken.' She turned to go, but couldn't resist a parting remark over her shoulder. 'That's an old familiar ploy,' she said, and with measured steps walked across the room away from him as sedately as she could.

As soon as she was safely out of the dining room, out of sight of those piercing grey eyes, Wendy, still seething, stalked across the lobby, her cheeks burning with humiliation and rage.

That horrible man, she thought as she started up the staircase. To create such a scene in public! And all over nothing. '*Damn* him,' she muttered to herself. She stood for a moment on the staircase, her fists clenched at her sides, glaring mindlessly in front of her.

She felt a hand on her arm and whirled around, ready to do battle again. It was Meg.

'Hey,' she said softly. 'What's wrong?'

'That man,' Wendy sputtered helplessly. 'That awful man!'

Meg took one look at her stricken face and began to steer her gently but firmly up the stairs to Wendy's room. Once inside, she sat quietly on the bed while Wendy poured out the story of Burke Flint and his terrible accusations.

'I'm tempted to pack my bags and leave the hotel,' she said finally. 'I don't think I can bear even to breathe the same *air* as that despicable egomaniac. Meg, I can still hardly believe my ears. To imagine that I would plot and plan a meeting with him to get him into *bed*, for heaven's sake, when that's the furthest thing from my mind with *any* man, much less an arrogant, overbearing, bad-tempered monster like Burke Flint.'

Gradually, as she paced the room, telling Meg what had happened, she began to feel calmer. She deliberately left out the part about the episode on the beach the night before. As far as she was concerned, that never happened.

'Attractive, is he?' Meg asked finally.

Wendy's eyes widened. 'What's that got to do with it?' she asked. 'Yes, I guess he's physically attractive—but pure poison underneath.'

'Well, I think you'd be crazy to leave,' Meg announced firmly. 'You have as much right here as he does.'

Wendy walked over to the window. The beach lay to the north of the hotel, so that the afternoon sun was to her left, just now setting in the western sky, filling it with a brilliant reddish glow. The palm trees swayed gently, and she could almost hear the lapping of the surf as it broke on the sandy beach.

She turned around. 'You're right. I can't leave. I won't let him spoil my vacation. I'll manage to stay out of Mr Burke Flint's way. I'll have my table changed first thing in the morning,' And, she added

to herself, I will certainly never swim on that particular stretch of beach again.

'Attagirl,' Meg cheered. 'There are plenty of
places to go where you won't run into him. Besides,
if he values his privacy so much, chances are he
won't be around underfoot, anyway.'

'I certainly hope not,' Wendy said. Just thinking
about him and his dreadful accusations made her
angry all over again. She could see again that tall
figure looming over the table, those steely grey
eyes fastened on her as though she had stolen the
crown jewels, for heaven's sake. She began to
giggle.

'I just hope he got his trousers good and soaked,'
she said, recalling the overturned glass of water.

'Serves him right,' Meg loyally agreed. 'Men!'
She stifled a yawn and got up from the bed. 'Sorry,
Wendy, I've got to go. It's been a long day and
tomorrow I start work.'

Wendy was so grateful to Meg for listening, for
understanding, for supporting her, that she felt a
reluctance to see her go.

'Can you stay just a little longer?' she asked.

'Sure, I guess so.' Meg sat back down on the bed
and gave Wendy a curious look. 'What's up?'

Wendy hesitated. She didn't want to jeopardise
their friendship, a friendship that was becoming
more valuable to her all the time, but she felt she
owed Meg the truth about her past. Then it was up
to Meg. She took a deep breath and plunged ahead.

'You asked me a question this morning,' she
began, 'a question I didn't want to answer.'

Meg gave her an odd look. 'I remember,' she said
slowly. 'I asked you if the man you'd been involved

with was married. I'm not sure I want to hear the answer, now.'

'Well, here it is, anyway,' Wendy said. 'Yes. He was married. But I didn't know he was when I met him, and the minute I found out—not very pleasantly—I broke it off. Permanently.'

'Why did you do that?'

Wendy could only stare. 'Why? What else could I do? How could we build a relationship on someone else's unhappiness?'

'Didn't he tell you they were on the verge of divorce anyway?' Meg asked drily.

'How did you know?'

Meg shrugged. 'Just a guess. It's been known to happen.'

'Well, yes, he did,' Wendy admitted. 'But,' she went on, 'that made no difference. If I hadn't come along they might have been able to work out their differences.'

She couldn't help noticing the hurt look on Meg's face. And I'm the one who put it there, she thought. She started to pace the floor again. 'Look,' she said, 'maybe I was wrong to tell you. You look as though I'd just slapped you, and I feel terrible. I never wanted to hurt you, only to be honest.'

Meg gave her a searching look. She seemed to be struggling with herself inwardly for a moment. Then she smiled. 'Sit down,' she said gruffly. 'Please. I thought I was over the worst of it. Obviously, I'm not as tough a character as I like to make out.' She sighed. 'I don't blame you. I knew right from the beginning, on the plane, that you'd been hurt, too. You develop a kind of sixth sense about that when you've been through it yourself. You've probably done the same thing I have, tried to bottle it all up inside and tough it out, the big strong character that never let's anyone see them shed a tear. Why don't you tell me about it? It might make us both feel better.'

Wendy sighed. 'There's not much to tell. We met, we fell in love, I found out he was married, that was the end of it. An old story, and not a very pretty one.'

'I'm curious,' Meg said. 'How did you find out?'

Suddenly Wendy wanted to talk about it, for the first time. The things she could never have confided in Greta she found herself eager to tell Meg. Why? Because she would understand.

'Actually, it was a pretty tame affair. I have a room-mate, so we really weren't alone all that much. I mean, it never got beyond the point of a few kisses—you know what I mean.'

'Sure,' Meg agreed, 'and he couldn't very well take you home with him—not with a poor unsuspecting wife lurking in the background. Why didn't you go away with him?'

'Well,' Wendy hesitated, 'I'm not very—experienced—with that kind of thing. I've never—you know.' Meg's eyes widened in disbelief and Wendy reddened. She hurried on. 'Anyway, I finally did agree to go away with him. I'm sorry, Meg, but I really did love him, and thought he loved me, and I had no idea he was married.'

'Go on,' Meg said. 'This is fascinating.'

'Well,' Wendy continued, swallowing, 'I knew he was a salesman for a company that manufactured heavy equipment, but I never knew where he lived or where his office was. We'd only known each other a few months. I'd had to work late the night we were to leave for a weekend at Ocean Shores and needed to get in touch with him to let him know. There were three David Warrens in the book. I tried the first one.'

Wendy would never forget that phone call. Even now, over the worst of it, able to talk about it at last, she still could feel that rush of blood to her face, the humiliation and anger. She paused for a while, not speaking, until she had herself under control again.

'When the woman answered the phone, my first thought was that I'd got the wrong David Warren. I was about to tell her I'd dialled the wrong number, but something made me decide to pursue it.'

She sat silently, then, remembering. Cautiously she had asked for Mr Warren. The woman had hesitated.

'This is his wife,' she had said, her voice suspicious. 'Who's calling?'

Instinct had warned Wendy to be cautious.

'This is his office,' she had lied, hating herself, but driven by the need to protect herself.

'Oh,' the woman had said. 'Just a minute.'

Wendy had waited holding her breath, hardly daring to move, her heart pounding wildly, a horrible buzzing sound in her ears. It can't be, she had thought. It won't be my David. Please, God, don't let it be my David.

But it was.

'Hello,' came the warm familiar voice, and Wendy's whole world had come crashing down around her.

'Goodbye, David,' she had said clearly—and then collapsed as soon as she had hung up.

Meg's voice broke in on her bitter memories. 'Well?' she was saying. 'What happened then?'

'I called his house to tell him I'd be late. His wife answered. I said goodbye and that was that.'

'But didn't he try to explain?' Meg asked.

'Oh, sure. He came right over. He tried to explain. I wouldn't listen.' She shuddered, remembering.

'You lied to me,' she had kept repeating stonily. 'You deceived me.'

'Listen,' Meg was saying, 'forget it. I can see this is upsetting you.'

Wendy stared at her. 'I felt unclean, Meg, somehow corrupted by the affair. I hated myself, hated David. Yet part of me still loved him, still wanted him. I couldn't get him out of my mind.'

'I know,' Meg said softly. 'They can do that to you. How about now? Is it over?'

Wendy thought a minute. 'I think so,' she said hesitantly. 'I hope so. It doesn't hurt now when I think of him.'

They sat in silence for a while, each absorbed in her own thoughts. Then they looked at each other. Meg smiled.

'A friend of mine made me do that after my divorce.'

'What?'

'Open up like that, spill it all out. I hope the operation was a success.'

Wendy returned the smile. 'I think maybe it was. I still seem to be all in one piece at any rate. Maybe one day I'll meet a nice, steady, dull man.' One who would not set her pulses racing or turn her bones to jelly, she thought. A man who would give her a home, quiet affection, security, children.

'Is that what you want?' Meg asked.

'Don't you?'

'Nope,' she said positively. 'Why should I settle for safety? Although it'll be a long time before the walls come down.' She stood up, then stretched and yawned. 'Now, I've really got to get to bed before I drop.'

It wasn't until Meg left that Wendy recalled Burke Flint's last words to her. The significance of them was inescapable. She had been too angry before to grasp that he was telling her he had remembered her from the night before, had recognised her. Not, however, until he had seen her bare shoulders when the shawl had slipped from them.

It was bad enough, she thought, that he had the idea she was out to trap him into a relationship of some kind where she could 'use' him, but the prospect of an actual involvement with such a man was unthinkable. As far as ruthlessness and male egotism went, he left David Warren decidedly in the shade.

What had he said? He had found that fame was a potent aphrodisiac. Wendy could well believe that. And even though she detested him, she had to admit that he was a very attractive man, with his slim muscular build, that shock of dark unruly hair and a certain air of authority and confidence he wore like a second skin. There was probably no shortage of women anxious to share his bed. But she wasn't one of them.

Later that night, after she had gone to bed, Wendy had to admit the whole episode did have its humorous side. His arrogance was so blatant it was almost endearing. He had looked so funny sitting there, eyes blazing, the water dripping on to his trousers. She would never dare face him again after that.

As she lay there, she began to put together bits and pieces she had heard and read about Burke Flint. Now that she knew who he was she could recall seeing him briefly on television during an interview. Then she remembered a *New Yorker* or *Time Magazine* article about him.

It seemed to her that he had been trained as a lawyer, but had never practised. Hadn't he inherited a lot of money? No, she thought, that must have been someone else. She did recall that his travels had taken him to some of the hottest trouble spots in the world, and that his columns were a regular feature in several newspapers.

So, she thought wryly, as she lay in the dark staring up at the ceiling, aside from being handsome, bad-tempered, arrogant, talented and famous, and possibly rich, he was just an ordinary mortal.

She had to laugh at that, as she turned over and settled down to go to sleep. The more she found out about Burke Flint, the more determined she was to stay as far away from him as possible.

CHAPTER THREE

'WELL, how do you like your new dinner partner by now?' Meg asked.

'He's a dear,' Wendy replied, 'a retired college professor whose wife died recently.'

It was three days later, and the two girls were sunbathing on the public beach they had discovered within walking distance of the hotel. They had formed the habit of going up there to swim after dinner, just before the sun went down. It was cooler then, with a little breeze off the sea.

'What does he look like?' Meg asked, rolling over on her back.

'Oh, he's got wispy white hair, a paunch and at last count seven grandchildren.'

'My, that sounds thrilling,' Meg commented drily.

'Not very thrilling, but he's sweet. And very good company.'

'And safe?'

Wendy looked at her and smiled. 'Quite safe.'

'How about the terrible Mr Flint? Have you seen him?'

'Only from a distance. I asked for a table as far away from his as possible. And, believe me, I've stayed out of his way.'

'He's in one of the cottages, isn't he?' Meg asked. 'That means he's not wandering around the hotel where you might bump into him, anyway.'

'Thank goodness for that,' Wendy said.

'By the way,' Meg remarked, 'I asked my boss, Mr Patera, about your Mr Flint.'

Wendy arched her eyebrows and opened her mouth. '*My* Mr Flint,' she protested. 'He's hardly that!'

Meg stretched lazily. 'Oh, you know what I mean. Anyway, Mr Patera went on and on about him, how honoured the hotel was to have such a distinguished guest, how he was going to win the Pulitzer Prize for his book about Vietnam, how I was to give him—and I quote our illustrious manager—"every consideration and service he might require."'

Wendy laughed. 'That covers a lot of territory. Just what "service" does Mr Patera have in mind?'

Meg sniffed. 'Not what you're thinking. Apparently, Mr Flint has no needs in *that* department. Mr Patera was also quite clear on that score.'

'What do you mean?' Wendy was curious, in spite of herself.

'Well, as Mr Patera delicately put it, "Mr Flint occasionally entertains a guest in his cottage." He made it clear that my services would be strictly secretarial. In other words, hands off.'

Wendy felt a sickening feeling in the pit of her stomach that could only be described as disappointment. Then she told herself she was being silly. Of course a man like Burke Flint would have relationships with women. It had nothing to do with her. That night on the beach meant nothing to either of them, nothing at all. His treatment of her the next night at dinner was proof of that.

Still, she was curious. 'Is there any one "guest" in particular?' she asked in a casual tone. 'Or is he more democratic than that?'

Meg didn't reply immediately, and without looking at her, Wendy was uncomfortably aware that Meg was staring at her. She could have bitten her tongue out for asking, but it was too late to take it back now.

'Well,' Meg said carefully, 'there hasn't been anyone so far, but I'll let you know when one appears.'

'Oh, don't bother,' Wendy said lightly. 'It has nothing to do with me.'

'No,' Meg said, 'I can see that.'

Wendy jumped to her feet. 'I think I'll go for a swim before the sun goes down. Coming?'

'Oh, I can't,' Meg said with a frown. She stood up and began to collect her things. 'The other short-hand-typist quits today, and I have a lot of work to catch up on tonight.'

'What happened?'

'Who knows? She was complaining about the heat one day, and the next she was giving her notice. The hotel's air-conditioned, so I don't know what her problem was. Anyway, there's a lot more work to do with her gone. I'd rather be busy, but I'm not sure I'll be able to cope for long all by myself.'

After Meg left, Wendy swam for a while by herself, then walked back to the hotel in the gathering dusk. The breeze had died down and the heat was becoming oppressive. She hurried, anxious to get back into the coolness of the hotel.

When she stepped inside the lobby, it seemed

warmer than usual, without the overpowering blast of cold air that usually hit her when she came in from outdoors. By the time she reached her room she had begun to perspire, even in the scanty bathing suit. Ordinarily she would have been shivering by now.

Something must be wrong with the air-conditioning, she thought, and reached down under the window to put a hand over the vent. Instead of the usual rush of cool air blowing out there was nothing, not even the flicker of a breeze. She listened for a moment, then realised that the low hum of the air-conditioning was missing. The room was quite silent.

She opened the window. The air outside seemed even warmer and stickier than in the room, and she shut it quickly. Perhaps it would cool off as it got darker, she thought, and she could open the window then. Her small room would be stifling before long.

She went into the bathroom, stripped off her bathing suit and got under a lukewarm shower. When she turned off the water she could hear the telephone ringing in the bedroom.

She wrapped herself in a large bath towel and ran into the next room. It seemed even warmer than before, in spite of the cooling shower. She picked up the receiver of the telephone, wondering who in the world could be calling her.

'Hello.'

'Miss Fuller, this is the hotel switchboard. We're notifying all guests that there is some trouble with the air-conditioning and we hope to have it repaired within an hour or two.'

'Thank you for telling me,' Wendy replied. 'I thought something must be wrong.'

She started to hang up when the voice continued. 'I have a long distance call for you, miss. Please hang on.'

Wendy waited. It was probably Greta, she thought, wondering how the healing process was progressing. Poor Greta. She'd had to bear the brunt of the turmoil of the past month, blaming herself for the whole thing. Now that I'm really on the mend, Wendy thought, I'll have to make it up to her in some way, at least reassure her the worst was over.

'Go ahead, please,' came the operator's voice.

'Hello,' Wendy said again.

'Wendy? Is that you? Darling, what have you done?'

Wendy gasped. It was David. How had he found her? What could she say to him? Her heart began to pound, and she considered simply slamming down the receiver.

She resisted the impulse, and slowly her pulse returned to normal and she could answer him calmly.

'Hello, David,' she said. 'How did you find out where I was?' Too many people had known, she thought. Greta was not famous for her discreet tongue, and a few girls at the bank, as well as her boss, had known, too.

'That doesn't matter,' he said impatiently. 'Why have you done this, gone off without a word? Don't I mean anything at all to you? I have a right to know when you just calmly decide to leave town.'

'Oh, David,' she said wearily, 'come off it. You

have no rights at all where I'm concerned. Please, just leave me alone.'

'But, damn it, I love you,' he shouted.

For a moment she weakened. David, in his way, really had loved her. She knew that. Even though he had deceived her about his marriage, he could never have simulated the love he showed her.

'I know, David,' she said softly, 'I know. But if you do, let me go now. There's no future for us. You know that.'

'I told you we were on the verge of divorce, anyway,' he said in a pleading tone. 'I just need a little more time to get things sorted out.'

'David,' she said patiently, 'I've said it a hundred times and I'll say it just once more. I will not be the cause of breaking up anyone's marriage. I could never live with myself.'

'But you were never the cause. It was on the rocks before you ever came into the picture. Don't you believe me?' He sounded desperate, and she almost felt sorry for him.

'Yes, I do,' she said truthfully. 'I may not have been the cause of your problems with your wife, but if I hadn't come along you might have worked them out. If you had told me the truth, you know, I would never have gone out with you.'

'I know that,' he groaned. 'I was terrified of losing you. That's the only reason I lied. You've got to believe me.'

Wendy's head began to whirl. They had been through this so many times. He still had the power to upset her, to confuse her, but this time she had had a month to find herself again, to get him out of her system. She knew she had no choice. They could never build a life together on the foundation of his wrecked marriage, not when she was the catalyst that had finally doomed it.

She *knew* she was right, and that knowledge gave her strength. If she were to give in to him now, the month of suffering would have been wasted. The decision was made. There was no turning back.

'I believe you, David,' she said gently, 'but it makes no difference. It's over between us. Please don't call me again.'

'Wendy, you've got to give me a chance,' he pleaded.

'Goodbye, David,' she said softly, and she hung up the phone.

She sat for a long time, her hand on the receiver, unmoving. Tears came to her eyes as she thought of David. In spite of the overwarm room, Wendy shivered. She felt bereft, lonely. Hearing David's voice had affected her deeply.

She had to admit to herself that she still felt drawn to him. He was a powerfully attractive man, and she had been ready for love. She had been relatively inexperienced at twenty-five, and David had been the man to awaken the banked fires within her.

She took a deep breath. The worst had passed. The telephone conversation, David's pleading, her own memories—all had unnerved her momentarily. She promised herself that she would never let herself become that vulnerable again. It had been a painful lesson, and one she wasn't likely to forget.

It was still hot in the small bedroom, and growing warmer by the minute. Wendy crossed over to the window and opened it. It seemed to be a little cooler outside, but without a cross-draught or a breeze, it didn't do much good.

Suddenly, through the open window, came the sound of music. Wendy listened and heard the steel band in the lounge. The mellow tones of the strange instruments were playing an island song, lilting and catchy. Then a man started to sing. Wendy knew it was probably the young vocalist whose picture was in the lobby near the lounge. He was a handsome native, tall, with a rich baritone voice.

She strained her ears to listen to the words of the song, but the lounge was too far away. On an impulse, she decided to go downstairs. If she could get away for an hour or two, she reasoned, perhaps the fresh air from the open window would cool off the stuffy room. She could sit in the lobby, and order a cool drink.

She put on her coolest dress, the black, low-cut sundress she had worn a few nights ago, locked her bedroom door behind her and started down the main staircase to the lobby. As she descended, the music became louder and she could hear the sound of voices drifting up, low conversations punctuated by subdued laughter.

The lobby was milling with people, so that even if it had been cooler, the mingling bodies would have raised the temperature. Wendy glanced around and saw that almost every available chair was taken. Women were fanning themselves with magazines and newspapers, and all the men seemed to be tieless and in shirtsleeves.

She decided to cross the lobby to the back entrance that led to the beach, hoping it would be a little cooler. In order to do so she had to walk past the lounge. As she passed by, she couldn't resist a peek inside.

Even though the interior of the lounge was dimmer than the lobby, Wendy could see clearly that here, too, all the men were in shirtsleeves, and many of them tieless. Apparently the edict against casual wear had been lifted by the management in view of the failure of the air-conditioning.

The vocalist, Richie Delamore, was singing a plaintive traditional love song. Entranced, Wendy stood for some time at the doorway, off to one side so she wouldn't block traffic going in and out. Richie Delamore had a fine true baritone with a lovely lilt to it that was perfectly suited to the native songs. The steel band accompaniment throbbed softly in the background. Wendy forgot the heat in the sheer enjoyment of the music.

She was jolted out of her reverie by a light touch on the back of her waist. Thinking she was in the way of someone wanting to go inside the lounge, she murmured a brief 'Sorry' and moved farther off to the side. When the touch not only lingered but pressed harder, she looked around, annoyed, wondering what the problem was. She found herself gazing into the grey eyes of Burke Flint.

Immediately she steeled herself for battle. Why couldn't he leave her alone? What was he going to accuse her of this time? Stationing herself at the lounge in the knowledge—or hope—that he would appear? She had gone out of her way to avoid him for three days and had thought she was safe from him.

She frowned and opened her mouth to make a cutting remark, but hesitated at the look on his face. He was actually smiling! She could hardly believe her eyes. Gone were the sarcastic sneer, the mocking frown, the hardness of the narrowed eyes. She gazed at him in disbelief, forced to admit to herself that he was quite attractive when he smiled. The lines of his jaw were still firm, the grey eyes still hard, but the mouth softened appealingly.

Wendy dropped her defences long enough at least to bite her tongue before starting a slanging match with him. Instead, she lifted her eyebrows inquiringly.

'Where have you been these last few days?' he asked. 'I've been looking for you.' He made it sound like an accusation.

'Why?' she asked in a sharp tone. 'Did you leave something out? I thought you covered every conceivable suspicion quite thoroughly.'

He held out a book. 'You left your book behind.' His smile widened, revealing strong, even white teeth.

'Somehow,' she replied icily, 'I've lost interest in it. However,' she said, reaching for it, 'since it was a *gift*, and not a deliberate plot to entrap you in some diabolical scheme, I guess I'd better have it back.'

She turned away from him, dismissing him, but his low voice continued, speaking to her from behind.

'Would you like a drink?' he asked softly.

She couldn't believe her ears. She turned around and gave him a suspicious stare. This was the man who only a few days ago had been accusing her of trying to trap *him* into paying attention to *her*. What had happened in the meantime to change his mind?

'I don't understand,' she replied at last.

'It's quite simple,' he said, frowning, and he perceptively stiffened. 'I merely asked you if you'd like a drink.'

Wendy couldn't help thinking how hard it must have been for him to make this gesture. He was obviously a proud man addicted to privacy and not getting much of it since he became such a celebrity. She gave him a wary glance. He was in his shirt-sleeves, a crisp white shirt with the cuffs rolled up, revealing strong forearms covered lightly with silky black hair. He had taken off his tie, too, and unbuttoned his shirt at the neck. His dark hair fell attractively across his forehead, giving him a boyish look that had not been evident at the dinner table when he had looked so severe and threatening. He even looked a little contrite, and she had to smile.

She really would like some company, and there could be no harm in having a drink with him.

'That's better,' he said. He put a hand on her waist. With his other hand he gestured towards the lounge. 'Shall we?'

'All right,' she said, 'if you're sure you'll feel safe with me.'

'Ouch,' he said wincing. 'I guess I asked for that.'

They found a free table not far from the band-stand where they could watch the show at close quarters. As he seated her at the table and went around to sit across from her, Wendy watched him, trying to understand what had caused this sudden change of heart in him. He had been so angry before.

During the show she stole an occasional surrepti-tious glance at him across the table, and she had to admit that Burke Flint was a compellingly attractive man. She told herself that wasn't why she had agreed to have a drink with him. Being with him here in the lounge with the music in the background, the other guests all around them chatting and laughing, seemed to her now a necessary aspect of the vacation, her own healing process, the reason why she had come to Nassau in the first place.

They sat silently together at the table for some time listening to the music, but it was not an uncomfortable silence. Burke Flint seemed the kind of man who would never be at a loss or ill at ease in any situation. He sat now in a relaxed posture, watching as the singer finished his number, his expression inscrutable but not forbidding. He seemed to Wendy a different man from that furious monster who had attacked her during their earlier hostilities.

He turned to her when the song was over. 'What would you like to drink? Are you the exotic type, a serious drinker or a wine connoisseur?'

'None of those, I'm afraid,' she replied with a smile. 'I hardly drink at all, but something cool would be very welcome.'

He beckoned to a hovering waiter and ordered two gin and tonics. Wendy liked the way he had deferred to her wishes, but, when he saw she had no serious preference, made the decision for her. David had been like that, she thought sadly. She waited for the terrible weight of regret and despair to descend on her at the very thought of David.

But this time it didn't. She glanced at Burke Flint and saw that he was staring at her intently.

'What's the matter with you?' he asked abruptly.

'What do you mean?' she said, surprised. She didn't think her momentary pang had been obvious.

He was frowning now, as if searching for an elusive fact. He cocked his head on one side. 'I'm not sure,' he said slowly. 'You're a very attractive girl, but I have the sense that you should be more than that. You remind me of a faded flower, or a blossom bowed down by rain. There's something not quite right about your looks.'

'Thanks a lot,' she said tartly. 'I may not be Miss Universe or a Playboy bunny, but I haven't quite reached the faded flower stage yet, I hope.'

'You know what I mean,' he said with an impatient gesture. 'What's your name, by the way?'

'Wendy. Wendy Fuller.'

'How old are you?' he asked.

She raised her eyebrows. 'How old are you?' she parried.

'Thirty-six,' he replied promptly. His eyes softened. 'I guess that was an impertinent question. It's the reporter in me, hot after the facts. Forget I asked.'

'I don't mind,' she said. 'I'm twenty-five.'

'Have you been ill?' he asked, frowning again. 'I don't know why, but I get the distinct impression of a beautiful girl who isn't quite up to par.'

She frowned slightly. 'Something like that.' There was a note of finality in her voice that he was quick to perceive, and he immediately changed the subject.

'Tell me about yourself,' he said in a more distant

tone. 'Are you married? Engaged? What kind of work do you do? Where do you live?'

She smiled. 'I'm neither married nor engaged. I work as a secretary in a bank, and I live in Baltimore. Did you invite me in here so you could interview me?'

'No,' he said, dropping his bantering tone and giving her a searching look. 'I invited you in here because I wanted to get to know you better. You intrigued me the other night.'

'You mean because I spilled water on you?' she asked mischievously. 'I'm really sorry about that. It wasn't deliberate.'

He waved a hand. 'That doesn't matter. I probably deserved it.' He rested his elbows on the table and leaned closer to her. 'You intrigued me first of all because of the way you fought back. A girl with less spirit would have slunk away in mortification, wanting to avoid a scene at all costs, but you stood your ground. I was out of line, by the way, with my accusations. I'm afraid I've become gun-shy with this damned celebrity status of mine.'

Wendy couldn't help wondering if his problem was entirely due to being a celebrity. She doubted if he had ever had much trouble finding feminine companionship.

'I take it,' she said, 'that you came to Nassau to get away from the limelight.'

'Partly,' he admitted. 'That's why I was so rude at dinner the first time. Then the next night when I saw my book in your hands, I just saw red. I think it was partly disappointment.'

'I don't understand,' she said.

He leaned farther across the table and looked

directly into her eyes. 'I told you. You intrigued me. Even before I recognised you from the beach the night before when I thought you were a mermaid, there was something about your looks, your whole bearing, that first night at dinner that interested me.'

She looked away. 'You're embarrassing me.' It was all happening too fast. Her mouth felt dry and little warning signals were going off in her head. The man was too attractive. He was very unlike David in looks, but his manner was similar—a compelling masculinity, an almost arrogant self-confidence that threatened to blind her to the fact that she was determined not to succumb to that kind of mindless infatuation ever again.

Just then their drinks arrived. It had become a little cooler in the lounge as it got darker outside, and a slight breeze had sprung up. Still, it was quite warm, and Wendy sipped on her cooling drink gratefully. The music had started again, and she began to relax, relieved that Burke Flint had dropped the touchy conversation after her last remark.

'Would you care to dance?' he asked, rising from his seat in anticipation of her assent.

Wendy hesitated. Nervously she took another swallow of her drink. She glanced at him and flushed as she saw the expression on his face. She had caught him just as his eyes had flicked briefly downwards, then back to her face, and she was suddenly quite aware of how revealing the black cotton sundress was.

'All right,' she said in a low voice. Hurriedly, she finished her drink.

The next thing she knew she had risen from her seat and was being swept into his arms and on to the tiny dance floor. At his first touch she felt a weakness steal over her that she knew she had to resist. Vaguely, she suspected that she shouldn't have had such a potent drink when she wasn't used to it, or drunk it quite so fast, but it was too late for that now.

As they danced, silently, his strong arms supporting her, she realised how lonely she had been this last month and how much she had missed the touch of a man. Part of her warned that this was the drink talking—that and the wound that had been opened by her conversation with David on the telephone earlier in the evening.

'But another part of her didn't care. Somehow it seemed exactly right for her to be just where she was. She laid her head on his shoulder and gave herself up to the music and the sheer physical pleasure of being in this strong man's arms. His hold on her tightened, and she gave a little gasp as she felt his hand move from her waist to the bare flesh of her back, gently caressing, sensuous, thrilling.

A wave of dizziness passed over her, and she stumbled a little in his arms. She looked up at him apologetically and found his grey eyes fastened on her. Their eyes locked together. He pulled her even closer.

'What's wrong?' he murmured in her ear. 'Are you all right?'

'Yes,' she whispered. 'Just a little dizzy.'

'Would you like some fresh air? I think it's cooled off a little outside by now.'

'Yes, please,' she said, nodding. 'I'd like that.'
Anything, she thought, to clear her head.

He guided her deftly out of the lounge, past the other couples on the crowded floor and through the screen doors that led to a small garden.

Once outside, her head began to clear, and she felt better. They walked down one of the brick paths that wound around the shrubbery. The exotic scents of the tropical flowers were heavy on the night air, and the music drifting out from the lounge added to the romantic setting. Wendy felt happy and at peace. Burke didn't touch her, nor did he speak. They just ambled on in a comfortable silence until they came to the edge of the sandy beach.

He stopped, then, and turned to face her. Wendy looked up at him, her eyes wide. He was quite tall and she had to tilt her head back to see his face. There was a moon again, and some dim light from the Japanese lanterns scattered around among the palm trees. It was a magical night, a magical moment. There was a look in those grey eyes of tender longing, and Wendy was drawn to him in spite of the warning bell going off once more in the deeper recesses of her mind.

She watched, mesmerised, as the dark head bent towards her. She closed her eyes then and felt his firm mouth graze her lips lightly. The warning bell sounded again, but the kiss deepened slightly just at that moment, and the decision was taken out of her hands as her body took over from her mind and carried her along on a wave of passionate response.

She sighed beneath his mouth as the hands encircling her waist moved up around her rib cage, stopping just below the full thrust of her breasts beneath the thin cotton dress. She raised her arms instinctively to his shoulders, closed her eyes and ran her hands down along the strong-muscled arms and back up again. She could feel his lips moving in a half sigh, half groan as her fingers trailed along over his shirt.

She moved her hands to his back, running them over the supple muscles which seemed to shudder under her touch. She clasped the back of his neck, her fingers entwining in the crisp black hair.

He wrapped his arms tightly around her now, pulling her even closer, so that their bodies were fitted together, meeting in all the most sensitive places. He tore his mouth away from hers and pressed his cheek against her hair, murmuring in her ear.

'God, you're beautiful,' he said. His breath came heavy and rasping. 'I want you, Wendy. Such a frail little girl.' His hands moved again over her slenderness, then abruptly came around and settled over her breasts. 'But definitely a woman.'

Wendy felt as though she was drowning. In all her time with David, their lovemaking had never progressed so far, nor had her response been so mindless, so violent. She loved the feel of Burke's large strong hands on her breasts, the thin material of her dress sliding sensuously over her bare skin as his hands moved rhythmically to caress her, the gentle fingers stroking the exposed flesh above the low neckline.

She drew in her breath sharply as one hand slipped inside the loose bodice to grasp a bare breast, his fingers circling the now hardened and

THE SCENT OF HIBISCUS 69

taut nipple. He reached up and slid the thin strap from her shoulders so that the breast was exposed. Wendy threw her head back, her eyes closed, giving herself up to the ecstasy of the moment as his mouth descended again on hers, forcing her head back even farther.

Then the other strap came down and she felt his fingers fumbling with his shirt. Then his arms were around her again, stroking her back, and she was drawn close to him, her bare breasts crushed against his chest.

The heady sensation of flesh on flesh made her senses reel. His mouth was clamped on hers in a bruising, passionate exploration. His hands slid down to her hips, pulling her closer, so that she could feel his male hardness pulsing, thrusting.

Suddenly a shout went up from the lounge. Wendy drew back. People were calling loudly to each other inside, doors were being slammed. Wendy shook her head, confused and shaken. She looked up at Burke.

'What is it?' she whispered. 'What's wrong?'

He listened for a moment, his head turned away so that she gazed up at his strong profile. She thought she could never get enough of looking at him.

He laughed then, and turned back to her, giving her a light kiss. 'It's the air-conditioning. Apparently it's functioning once more.'

Hot with embarrassment now that the spell was broken, Wendy pulled up the straps of her dress and turned away. She couldn't face him. What must he think of her? What had got into her? Then she felt a strong hand grip her chin and force her head around so that she had to look up at him. Their eyes met. There was an amused look on his face.

'You're new to this kind of thing, aren't you?' he asked.

'Um,' she hedged, 'relatively so.'

She watched as he casually buttoned up his shirt and tucked it into his dark trousers. 'That's what I thought. Well, let's not rush things, shall we?' he asked lightly. 'I suppose you're a virgin.'

Wendy blushed fiery red. That subject had been a source of endless speculation and amusement to her friends. It was a touchy point with her, and she was immediately on the defensive.

Burke must have caught this by the look on her face, or the way she stiffened. He reached out a hand and put it gently on her cheek.

'Hey,' he said softly, 'it's okay. It's a good thing. A little unusual these days, that's all.'

He took her by the shoulders and pulled her to him once again. His hold on her tightened and she could feel his heart begin to beat faster. She put her hands on his chest and pushed back from him.

'Burke,' she said, saying his name for the first time, 'I've got to go to my room now. Alone. I'm afraid I'm way out of my depth. Everything has happened so fast. Just a few days ago you were shouting accusations at me. Now . . .' She shrugged and spread out her hands in a bewildered gesture. 'I just don't know.'

He put a hand on her neck, then slid it down over her shoulder, down her arm, then back up to rest lightly on her breast. She gasped at his touch and at the casual, offhand manner of the gesture.

'I could make you want to stay,' he murmured as

his fingers tugged gently, possessively at the bodice of her dress.

The thought leaped into her mind then that this was a very dangerous man. As if he could read her mind, he released the thin material and smoothed it down with his fingers, his hand brushing lightly across her breast as he did so.

'But I won't,' he said. 'You go back to your room and think things over.'

He was dismissing her as though she was a child, Wendy thought. Next he'll pat me on the head and tell me to be a good girl.

'Don't patronise me,' she said evenly. 'I may be sexually inexperienced, but I'm not stupid.'

He raised sardonic black eyebrows. There was a steely glint in the hard grey eyes, but his mouth quirked in amusement. 'You do get your feathers ruffled easily, don't you?' The eyes narrowed. 'Don't tempt me, Wendy. You'd better go before I change my mind.'

Annoyed, she turned away and started to walk up the path towards the hotel, but she stopped in her tracks when she heard him call her name.

'Wendy.' She turned around. 'I'm staying in one of the cottages. Alone. Number eight. Just in case.'

'Goodnight, Burke,' she said in a clear voice, and resumed her steps. His ironic laughter followed her until she was inside the hotel.

By the time she had made her way through the lounge and up the stairs to her room, Wendy was shaking uncontrollably. Safe in her room at last, she shut and locked the door behind her and leaned back against it, trembling from head to foot.

'What have I done?' she whispered aloud. She

pressed the back of one hand against her mouth so hard that her teeth bit into the inside of her lip.

Through the open window she could still hear the steel band playing in the lounge. She stumbled across the room and slammed it shut. Before she drew the blinds, she glanced down at the garden below, but the tall figure was nowhere to be seen.

For one panic-stricken moment she considered packing her bags and leaving the hotel. Surely she could find another room in town at this time of year. Still, why should she let him drive her away?

She sat down on the edge of the bed, trying hard to calm down and think. She knew she had been an utter fool to allow herself to become carried away like that with a man she hardly knew—with *any* man, for that matter. Bitterly she thought to herself that she deserved heartache and disappointment if that's the kind of fool she was going to make of herself whenever a man showed some interest in her.

Still brooding over her careless stupidity, she undressed, washed her face, slipped on a nightgown and sank wearily into her bed, her thoughts and senses still reeling.

She considered all the safe, serene years before David came along. Had he somehow marked her for life, awakening her so that from now on she would be vulnerable to every attractive man who came along?

She shuddered and flopped over on her stomach. What did she know about Burke Flint? What had possessed her to allow him such freedom of her body? She began to tremble again as she recalled the feel of those strong hands on her naked flesh, his warm mouth on hers.

'No, no, no!' she cried aloud, pounding her pillow with her fists. 'I will not allow this to happen to me.'

She turned on to her back again and gazed blankly up at the ceiling, willing herself to calm down. It all seemed so cheap now, she thought coldly. It was the drink, the music, David's phone call. She had been in a weakened condition.

Tomorrow, she thought, as she turned over once again. I'll think about it tomorrow. Finally, she drifted off to sleep, emotionally exhausted. Her last conscious thought was of a tall dark-haired man, his arms around her, his lips pressed on hers, and the unexpected response he had awakened in her.

CHAPTER FOUR

THE next morning Wendy awakened to the bright light of day with the firm conviction that, cowardly or not, she would have to leave. Burke Flint knew her name now, knew where to find her. She didn't think he would just leave her alone after last night, and she didn't trust herself to resist him.

As if to insure herself against a change of heart, she packed her bags as soon as she got up, then dressed in the same polka dot dress and navy blue jacket she had worn on the flight down.

On her way to the coffee shop for breakfast she stopped by at the desk and checked out. There, she thought, feeling better for having taken positive action, it's done, and it's for the best.

She ordered a hearty breakfast, and as she sat drinking her coffee and gazing out at the sunlit beach, her conviction began to waver. She thought of going back to Baltimore, to her job, the noisy dirty city, the dreary routine of getting up day after day, riding the crowded bus to work, the emptiness of the evenings and weekends without David.

No, she said firmly to herself, I'm leaving. It had to end soon anyway. She had already spent too much money as it was.

Her breakfast arrived, and as she ate the scrambled eggs and toast, her strength of will seemed to return. It wasn't only escape from Burke Flint, she rationalised. She had come here to get over David and was confident she had at least accomplished that, even though she had almost made just as big a mistake again. Burke Flint wasn't married, but she certainly could see no future with a man like him.

She looked up and saw Meg crossing the room towards her, and her spirits drooped again. She would miss the small redhead.

'You're up mighty early for a night-owl,' Meg said with a heavy sigh. She flopped down on a chair.

Wendy gave her a searching look, taking in the circles under her eyes, the weary droop of her shoulders and general air of exhaustion.

'You look as though you've taken to late hours yourself,' she said finally. 'Have some coffee.'

'Does it show that badly?' Meg asked. She poured herself some coffee and sighed again.

'What's wrong? I hope you're not coming down with some rare tropical disease.'

Meg snorted. 'I should be so lucky. At least I'd get some rest.' She raised her head with an effort and gave Wendy a sweeping glance. Then her eyes widened. 'Are you going somewhere?' she asked.

Wendy hesitated. Then, 'Yes, I am. I've decided to leave.'

'Today?' Meg asked in a bewildered tone. 'Back to Baltimore?'

'I'm afraid so.' She had thought out what she would tell Meg. She had made up her mind that she wouldn't lie to her, but neither did she need to tell her the whole truth. 'It's a simple matter of economics,' she went on. 'Even at summer rates, this hotel costs more than I can afford.' She smiled. 'I came here mainly to mend my broken heart, and I think I'm cured. I figured the money would be well-spent if I could accomplish that, but I really can't afford such an expensive vacation just for fun.'

Meg sipped her coffee in silence, brooding and frowning for some moments. Then she asked: 'Do you want to go back?'

Wendy laughed. 'Wanting doesn't enter into it, Meg. You know that. You have to earn your living, too. I don't even have a family to fall back on.'

'You mean you're an orphan?' Meg asked.

'Well, yes, I guess you could say that. My parents were both killed when I was a baby. I was raised by my grandmother, but she died too a few years ago.' She noticed the look of quick sympathy on Meg's face. 'It's okay, Meg,' she said softly. 'I'm used to being on my own. I don't know what it's like to have a family.'

'But if you had a choice,' Meg insisted, 'would you rather go back to Baltimore or stay here?'

Wendy frowned. 'I don't know how to answer that, Meg,' she said. 'Sure I'd rather stay here, but I can't, so I don't think about it.'

A light appeared in Meg's hazel eyes. She sat up in her chair and leaned across the table with a conspiratorial air.

'How would you like to stay on and work with me?'

Wendy could only stare, wide-eyed. Finally, she said, 'Meg, that's crazy. I can't do that.'

'I don't see why not,' Meg went on in a rush. 'You are a secretary, aren't you?' Wendy nodded dumbly. 'You know typing, shorthand, all that?' Wendy nodded again. 'Well?' Meg said, grinning and shrugging her shoulders, palms upraised.

'There's no problem. I've got to get some help or I'll drop. You don't really want to go back to Baltimore. We could have a great time.'

Wendy shook her head. 'It's not possible, Meg. I couldn't.'

'Give me a reason,' Meg persisted. 'One good reason.'

Wendy racked her brain. She had taken leave from her job at the bank for an indefinite period. Greta would be all right for the rent for a while. She didn't want to go back. Except for one thing—Burke Flint.

She shook her head. 'There are so many reasons, I can't even begin. I just can't.'

Meg sighed and shrugged. 'Well, I tried. If you want to go back, I guess there's nothing more I can say.' She was silent a moment. Then, 'Of course, the pay is good and there's free room and board.' Silence. 'And if you're worried about Burke Flint, you'd sleep and eat in the employees' quarters—which aren't bad. You'd never even see him.'

'I thought you said you had work to do for him,' Wendy rejoined quickly.

'I do, but I never see him. He dictates everything on tape and sends it up with one of the waiters.'

Wendy bit her lip and frowned. She was tempted. Why should she go back so soon? This might be a perfect solution for her. She would have a paid vacation and still be able to stay away from the dangerous Burke Flint.

'Well,' she said finally, 'I could maybe try it for a while. But just until you find someone else. It's only temporary, just so I can stay a little longer.'

Meg clapped her hands like a little girl, her face beaming.

'Mr Patera will be ecstatic,' she said happily. 'With all the extra work, he's been afraid I'd walk out on him, too.' She stood up. 'Are you through?' Wendy nodded. 'Well, let's go meet him, then.'

Mr Patera was a short, balding, harried-looking man somewhere, Wendy guessed, in his early forties. He was seated behind a huge wooden desk in the manager's office, dwarfed behind large piles of papers.

He gave Meg a suspicious, wild-eyed look when she came bursting into his office with Wendy in tow.

'Mr Patera,' Meg cried, 'you'll never guess what happened.'

He jumped to his feet and ran a hand over his sparse hair. 'You're not leaving,' he said with a fatalistic groan.

'Now, Mr Patera, would I do that to you?'

He rolled his eyes heavenwards and made a shrugging gesture, his hands spread helplessly. 'Why not? Everyone else does.'

Meg leaned across the desk and crowed triumphantly. 'I've found you another secretary. Meet my friend, Wendy Fuller.'

As if unable to believe in a piece of good news, Mr Patera glanced suspiciously from one girl to the other. Finally he spoke to Wendy.

'You want the job?' he asked.

'Well,' she began, 'just for a while until . . .'

'You're hired,' he said abruptly, and sat back down in his chair, dismissing them.

'But . . .' Wendy hedged.

He gave her a sharp look over a pile of papers. 'But what?'

'Well, you haven't even interviewed me,' Wendy said lamely.

'Can you type?' he snapped.

'Yes.'

'Take shorthand? Use a dictaphone?'

'Well, yes, but . . .'

He pointed to an open doorway in the wall beside his desk. 'Then go get to work. Meg can fill you in on details, show you your room.'

He went back to his papers, sighing and groaning. Meg beckoned to her, and Wendy followed her through the doorway into a small office with two typing desks.

'Here's our office,' Meg said with a sweeping gesture. 'Not bad, considering it's in the Caribbean with the beach in our back yard. Now, why don't we go get your bags out of your room and I'll show you your quarters.'

It only took an hour for Wendy to transfer her belongings from her room on the second floor to the employees' quarters on the main floor. She thought of calling Greta to let her know what had happened, but decided she'd wait until evening when the rates were cheaper. If Greta wanted to find her, she'd still be in the hotel.

Her room was pleasant and roomy, and even had a television set. Although there was no sea view, she did have her own bath. It was one large room, with a bed in a small alcove, so that it looked more like a sitting room than a bedroom. There was a comfortable couch, a coffee table, an end table

with lamp, a dresser and a desk with a good light.
The bathroom was spotless. Towels and linens
were supplied by the hotel, as well as all her laundry.

When she had unpacked and put her things
away, Wendy went back to the office she would
share with Meg to see if she could help her. Meg
was overjoyed at her appearance and immediately
brought her a pile of tapes with appropriate folders
indicating the name of the guest requesting the
work.

'Thank goodness you're here,' Meg said with a
heartfelt sigh. 'It's not as bad as it looks,' she added
hurriedly when she saw the look of dismay on
Wendy's face. 'Most of the tapes have only one
or two short letters on them. Even the execu-
tives spend most of their time here on vacation
from work, but there always seems to be the odd
matter that only a certain person can take care
of.'

'Do you use any particular format?' Wendy
asked, putting the top tape into the cassette-player
on her desk. 'What about stationery.'

'They give you all the directions you need on the
tape, and if there's special stationery it will be in the
file folder. Otherwise, just use plain bond paper.
There's plenty in the desk, along with carbon
paper, extra ribbons, and other supplies. You
won't have any trouble.'

Wendy put on the earphones and pressed her
foot on the pedal attached to the cassette-player.
Soon she was typing busily, glad in a way to be
getting back to work. As the morning progressed,
she became engrossed in the work, and she looked

up in surprise when Meg planted herself in front of her typewriter, arms folded, smiling.

'You don't have to do them all today, you know,' Meg said. 'It's time for lunch.'

Wendy glanced at her watch. 'Twelve-thirty,' she exclaimed. 'I can hardly believe it.'

'Are you hungry?'

'Starved. Where do we eat?'

'We have lunch and breakfast in the coffee shop, dinner in the employees' dining room just across the hall from the kitchen. We take what we're given, but it's usually good. Nothing fancy, and no great choices, but better than the usual institutional food.'

In the coffee shop they ordered sandwiches and small salads. Wendy flexed her back muscles, which had become a little stiff from the unaccustomed bending over the typewriter.

'Well,' Meg said, 'what do you think?'

'I think it's great,' Wendy replied. 'Much more interesting than what I do at home.'

'Banks are pretty dull, I imagine,' Meg said, making a face.

'My department isn't so bad. It's the business extension section. They try to get new business for the bank, and there is a variety of clients, so it's not always the same old thing. But, still, it's fascinating to have something entirely different on each tape.'

'Wait until you do one of Burke Flint's,' Meg said, rolling her eyes. 'He's writing a new book, and he really has the gift of the gab. The words just come rolling out. I have a real problem keeping up with him.'

'I can imagine,' Wendy replied drily. Their sandwiches arrived and Wendy ate hungrily. 'What's the new book about?' she asked between bites.

'Poland—you know, the problems the union is having with the Communists there,' Meg replied. 'I know that sounds kind of dull, but he really makes it fascinating.'

'I'm sure he does.' She remembered the book on Vietnam that Greta had given her, still lying unread in her suitcase.

Meg sighed. 'The only problem is, I have to do everything twice for him.'

'Why's that?' Wendy asked. They had finished lunch and were on their way back to the office. 'Does he do a lot of revising?'

'No, not a lot,' Meg said, seating herself at her desk. She gave Wendy a rueful grin. 'It's my spelling. I'm a terrible speller, always have been.' She brightened. 'I'm good at punctuation, though.'

Wendy laughed and sat down at her typewriter. 'Well, that's something. Why not use the dictionary?'

Meg shrugged. 'I did for a while when the other secretary was here, but since she left I just haven't had the time. Besides he uses such a lot of big words I've never heard of.' She gave Wendy a calculating look. 'How about you?'

'Hmm?' Wendy asked. She had been examining the work stacked up on the desk before her.

'How's your spelling?'

'It's okay,' Wendy replied idly. She slipped a tape into the cassette-player and reached for the earphones.

Meg gazed at her thoughtfully for a few seconds while Wendy fiddled with the buttons on the cassette-player.

Meg cleared her throat loudly. 'Maybe you could do Burke Flint's tapes, then,' she said. Wendy gave her a startled look and Meg rushed on, 'You'd never even have to see him or talk to him. All he does is send the tapes up here every morning with the waiter, and I send the typed pages back when I'm done.'

Wendy frowned. She wanted nothing whatsoever to do with Burke Flint. He terrified her. She had allowed him to get too close to her as it was. She sensed that if he ever had any power over her she'd be lost. Her experience with David was still too fresh in her mind to ever risk that again.

'I'd rather not,' she said slowly.

Meg shrugged and sighed loudly. 'Well, I won't push you, but I think you're being silly. You'd enjoy it. He's a good dictator, and the book is fascinating. He never comes to the office. I've never even seen him. He'd never know who was doing the typing.'

Wendy slowly raised her eyes to meet Meg's pleading gaze. I'm probably being silly, she thought. Besides, what better way to prove to myself that he means nothing to me than to do his work?

'Well,' she said, 'if you're sure I won't have to meet him.'

'Oh, thanks a million, Wendy,' Meg said happily. 'You're a real pal.'

She brought over the pile of tapes to Wendy's desk and carried the files and tapes Wendy had started back to her own. They both worked steadily through the afternoon until finally Wendy noticed Meg give a long sigh. She looked over from her typewriter.

'Five o'clock,' Meg said, grinning. 'I do believe I begin to see daylight in this mess. How are you doing?'

The afternoon had flown by for Wendy. She had to admit that working for Burke Flint was far more interesting than anything else she had ever done. He was a superb dictator, his voice low, firm and steady, just slow enough so that she could keep up with him, but never dragging.

'I'm doing fine,' she replied. 'You were right. It's a very interesting book.'

'He sounds like a very interesting man, period,' Meg remarked drily. 'If he looks anything like he talks, I think you must be out of your mind to try to keep away from him.'

Wendy shivered a little. 'Meg, the very thought of getting involved again with a man like Burke Flint sends chills up and down my spine. Believe me, I know what I'm doing. He's a dangerous man.'

'Oh, I know,' Meg said, rolling her eyes. 'Don't I wish I could meet a dangerous man.'

Wendy was incredulous. 'After what you've been through?' she asked. 'You must be a glutton for punishment.'

Meg shrugged. 'What do you get out of life by playing it safe?'

'I'll tell you,' said Wendy firmly. 'You get peace of mind.'

'Peace of mind isn't everything,' Meg said, a challenge in her voice. 'Sure, I got hurt, but it's a funny thing—I wouldn't give up a minute of my marriage to that big jerk. He was what I wanted, and I had him for a little while, anyway.'

Wendy could only stare. 'You mean you think the whole thing was worth it? I can't believe you, Meg.'

Meg shrugged and began to put the cover on her typewriter. 'Well, it's true.' She gave Wendy a searching look. 'You may be able to hide from the Burke Flints of this world, the Davids, the men like my husband, but you can't hide from yourself and your own feelings.'

Wendy flushed deeply. She knew there was truth in what Meg said, but the hurt was still too near, too raw. She turned her face and busied herself with putting pencils back in the drawer and straightening papers. When she looked up she had to smile at the contrite look on Meg's face.

'Hey,' Meg said, 'let's not argue about men, of all things. We're in this together, you know.' She sighed. 'Maybe I'm crazy—a perennial optimist— but I still believe in love.' She grinned. 'Let's go for a swim.'

Wendy was tired that night. After their swim at the public beach she and Meg had dinner in the employees' dining room. It was a filling meal, with large portions, and best of all, she thought, it was free. She went to her room alone after dinner, and after showering and putting on her robe and slippers she decided to call Greta. She owed her some kind of explanation for her decision, and while the phone rang she tried to piece together a plausible story that wouldn't quite be a deception yet left out any mention of Burke Flint.

'Hello.' Greta's familiar voice came on the line.

'Hi, Greta. It's me. Wendy.'

'Say, kiddo, I was about ready to call out the marines or something. I haven't heard a word from you for days. Not even a postcard.'

'I'm sorry, Greta,' Wendy said, instantly contrite. 'Things have been happening so fast that the time has flown.'

'Sounds interesting.' Greta waited, but when there was no response, she went on, 'I hope that means you're back in one piece.'

'Oh, yes,' Wendy said, laughing a little. 'The cure seems to be permanent.'

'Well, that's good to hear. No more tears for David, then?'

'David who?' Wendy replied firmly.

Greta chuckled delightedly. 'I believe you. For weeks I was afraid to even mention his name. In fact . . .' She hesitated.

Wendy waited for a long moment, but there was silence at Greta's end. 'Greta?' she said, wondering if the connection had been broken.

'I'm still here,' Greta replied slowly. 'Uh, Wendy,' she faltered, 'I don't suppose you've heard anything from him.'

'From David?' Wendy asked. 'Why, yes, as a matter of fact, he did call a few nights ago. Why?'

'Well, he was so insistent. Threatened to go to your boss. I'm sorry, Wendy, but I had to tell him where you were. I was so afraid he'd make a scene at the bank. He was like a wild man. I'm really sorry.'

'Hey, it's okay,' Wendy reassured her. 'Yes, he called, and I figured you must have told him where I was, but it was good for me to talk to him. It only confirmed my decision to make a permanent break with him.'

Greta sighed deeply. 'Thank goodness. I've been so worried about it, and I felt so guilty.'

'Well, you can forget it. No harm done—it's really over.' She paused a moment. 'Listen, Greta, the reason I'm calling is that I've decided to stay down here a while longer.'

'How much longer?' Greta asked. 'I thought you'd have run out of money by now.'

'I already have.' Wendy hesitated. 'I've just about made up my mind to take a job here, Greta,' she said at last. 'With the hotel, as a public typist.'

'A permanent job?' Greta asked in disbelief.

'Well, it started out as a temporary job, just to help out a friend. But if it works out, I might stay.' If I can keep away from Burke Flint, she added to herself. 'What I'm worried about,' she went on, 'is the apartment. I don't like to leave you out on a limb with the rent and expenses.'

'Oh, don't worry about that,' Greta replied, and Wendy thought she could detect a note of relief in her voice. 'A friend of mine has been staying here with me, and wants to move in permanently.'

Wendy smiled to herself. It was obvious that Greta's 'friend' was male. 'Well, that's fine, then,' she said. 'I'm glad you've found someone compatible.'

Greta chuckled. 'I never could fool you, could I?' she said. 'I know it's not your thing, but don't judge too harshly. I think this is really it. We've discussed marriage, but feel we should give living together a try first. You understand.'

'Of course,' Wendy said hurriedly. 'I'm happy for you, Greta. And relieved that I'm not leaving you in the lurch.'

'What about your job, though?' Greta asked. 'Aren't they keeping it open for you?'

What about my job, Wendy wondered. She hadn't really thought about that. To be fair, she should either go back soon or quit so that her boss could get a replacement for her.

'I'm not sure yet. As I said, if things work out here, I think I'd like to stay. The work is interesting, and it's so beautiful I hate to think of leaving.'

'I must say I wouldn't blame you for staying as long as you can. After all, a good secretary can always get a job, and if it doesn't work out for you down there you'll find something else. By the way, I read in the paper the other day that you had quite a celebrity staying in your hotel.'

Wendy's heart stopped, then began to pound violently. 'Oh, really?' she asked, trying to sound casual. 'Who's that?'

'Burke Flint. You know, the glamorous war correspondent. Remember, I gave you his book to read. I'm not surprised you didn't know he was there. Apparently he's gun-shy about publicity and tries to keep a low profile. According to the gossip columns he's quite a catch. Never been married, lots of money, and if the picture in the article was anywhere near the truth, he's gorgeous.'

Wendy only murmured non-committally in reply, neither denying she knew he was at the Emerald Beach nor volunteering that she knew him. There was no sense stirring Greta up, and she was determined to forget about Burke Flint at all costs, anyway.

'Well, let me know what you decide,' Greta said. 'It sounds good. At least send a postcard.'

Wendy promised she would keep in touch, and they said goodbye. She sat for a long time wondering if she had done the right thing—or was about to make a very foolish mistake.

Why should she go back? There was nothing for her in Baltimore. She had no family. She had decided to stay on in Baltimore when her grandmother died just because she had grown up there, had childhood friends there—Greta was one.

I'll give it a week, she thought. If I find at the end of a week that I still like it here and can avoid Burke Flint, I'll write to the bank and tell them I'm not coming back.

She climbed into bed then, and picked up the book she had put on the bedside table when she had unpacked that morning.

She couldn't resist a glance at the back cover, and her heart lurched at the sight of those piercing grey eyes in the photograph, the shock of dark hair, the flat planes of his cheeks, the thin mouth set in a forbidding line.

He was dressed in some sort of battle uniform, the rumpled shirt open at the collar, the sleeves rolled up above his elbows. He looked tired, and there was a cynical, almost bitter twist to his mouth. The eyes appeared to be focused on some unnamed horror.

As she gazed at the photograph, she found herself remembering the feel of his kisses, of his large sensitive hands on her body, the look of desire in the grey eyes out in the garden that night when he had held her.

She thought about Greta and her new roommate. She wondered what it would be like to live with a man you weren't married to, had made no commitment to. Greta could handle it, she thought. If it went wrong, she could shrug her shoulders and walk away from it, chalk it up to experience.

I wish I were more like that, she thought. Maybe there's something wrong with me. But she knew she could never cope with such a temporary relationship. She sighed and turned back to the book, opening it at the beginning. After a few pages, her eyes started to close. She put the book back on the table, switched off the light, and was soon sound asleep.

In the days that followed, Wendy and Meg established a pleasant working routine. They worked well together, and although different in temperament, got along quite well in a relationship that took the other's idiosyncracies into account without annoyance on either side.

Meg was impatient, volatile, and dashed through her work at a fast clip, speedily, although not always accurately. Wendy was more patient and meticulous. While she worked steadily on the seemingly limitless flow of tapes from Burke Flint, Meg handled the rest of the daily work that was sent to them.

By the end of the week, Wendy had made up her mind. She knew she wanted to stay in Nassau. They

were at their desks, steadily typing, when she realised she had already made her decision. She stopped typing and stared across at Meg.

'What is it?' Meg asked, aware of the scrutiny. 'Is
my lipstick smeared? Or have you had a sudden
revelation? Or are you just sick of those tapes?'

Wendy laughed. Far from being sick of Burke
Flint's tapes, she had found herself becoming more
deeply engrossed in the story every day. He had a
wonderful style, she thought, able to bring home
the poignancy of the terrible sufferings of the Polish
people through the centuries without ever once
lapsing into maudlin sentimentality. As the fine
reporter he was, he let the facts speak for themselves, stark and tragic enough without embellish-
ment.

'Not yet,' she replied. 'He's really quite a writer.'

'He must be,' Meg retorted drily, 'with all those
big words he uses. And the Polish names! I couldn't
keep them all straight.'

Wendy smiled. The names were difficult, but she
had noticed right away that he always spelled them
once, and she had drawn up a list in alphabetical
order to refer to.

'Some of them are a mouthful,' she agreed. She
hesitated. 'Meg,' she said slowly, 'do you think Mr
Patera would keep me on permanently?'

Meg stared at her open-mouthed for a moment,
then her whole face lit up. 'Do you mean it?'

Wendy nodded. 'I think I do,' she said.

Meg jumped up and ran to Wendy's desk, leaned
over, and began to gesture excitedly. 'You bet he'd
keep you on permanently. He'd jump at the
chance.'

Wendy waved a hand at the tapes piled on her desk. 'But this book won't go on forever. What about when it's finished? What then?'

'By then it'll be winter and the season here will just be getting started. There'll be plenty of work for the two of us. And, just think, in December, when Baltimore is freezing, you'll be basking on the beach in the Bahamas.'

Just as Meg had predicted, Mr Patera was delighted at Wendy's decision to stay on permanently. That was one out of his many problems in running the busy hotel that was settled satisfactorily.

That afternoon, summoning up all her courage, Wendy typed a brief letter to her boss at the bank in Baltimore, thanking him for keeping her job open for her, but explaining that the opportunity to work in the Bahamas was too tempting to pass up, and that she wouldn't be coming back to her old job.

When she finished the letter, she read it over several times, still hesitating. Finally, she signed her name, addressed and sealed the envelope, put on a stamp and walked firmly out into the lobby. At the mail slot, she took a deep breath, then slipped the letter inside.

There, she thought, as she walked back to the office, I did it. After one fleeting moment of panic at what she had done, she discovered that she felt quite pleased with herself.

'Well?' Meg said when Wendy returned. 'Did you actually do it?'

Wendy nodded, grinning. 'Yes. I did it.'

'How do you feel?'

'I feel great. I don't understand it—I should be quaking in my boots.'

'The reason you feel so good about it,' Meg said in a decisive tone, 'is that you've actually made the move, burned your bridges. You were so twitchy before because of the indecision.'

Wendy opened her eyes wide. 'Meg, you constantly amaze me. How did you come by such wisdom?'

Meg grimaced ruefully. 'The hard way, my friend,' she replied flatly. 'That seems to be the only way.'

It was the next day that Wendy caught her first glimpse of Burke Flint since that night in the garden. She had wondered occasionally why she hadn't seen him, but the steady flow of tapes he sent to be typed indicated that he was working long hours on his book. Besides, she was either in the office working or in the employees' quarters. She and Meg only swam on the public beach.

It was in the coffee shop at noon that she saw him. Meg had stopped to talk to Mr Patera, and Wendy had gone ahead to the coffee shop. She was standing at the entrance looking around the room for a table when it happened. He had just finished his lunch and was getting up from his table. He had a book with him and was standing with his back to the window, on Wendy's right.

She drew in her breath sharply at the sight of him. Her heart began to pound and a wave of dizziness passed over her. She knew she should make a beeline out of there before he saw her, but she stood transfixed, one hand at her throat, unable to move.

He was so tall, she thought, staring at him. The strong clean lines of his profile were outlined against the bright glare from the windows, a lock of the dark hair falling across his forehead. He was dressed casually in tight dark trousers and a white knitted shirt that clung to the powerful muscles of his chest and shoulders.

There was an arrogance, Wendy thought, an air of total self-assurance, just in the way he stood, the way he bent his head, the way he reached into his trouser pocket to take out a tip for the waitress.

Just in time, Wendy came to her senses, and backed away from the entrance behind the curtain, out of his line of vision. Had he seen her? She stood for a moment, trembling, then turned to run away, colliding head-on with Meg.

Meg grabbed her by the shoulders. 'Hey, hold on. Is the place on fire?'

'Let me go,' Wendy muttered through her teeth, in a panic now that she had regained her senses. 'I've got to get out of here.'

Meg dropped her hands from Wendy's shoulders and held her by the arm, peering into her face. 'What's wrong, Wendy?' she asked with concern in her voice. 'You look as though you've seen a ghost.'

'In there,' Wendy choked, pointing. 'In the coffee shop. It's Burke Flint. I've got to go before he sees me.'

Still hanging on to her arm, Meg drew back the edge of the curtain and glanced inside. When she turned back to Wendy, her eyes were wide.

'That's him?' she asked with something like awe

in her voice. 'That's Burke Flint? That tall, dark, gorgeous man in the dark trousers and white shirt?' Wendy nodded dumbly. 'That's the man you want to stay away from?' Meg's voice was incredulous. She shook her head. 'You must be out of your mind.'

Wendy pulled free of Meg's grip. 'Is he coming?' she asked.

Meg lifted the curtain again. 'No,' she said. 'He's going out the other way, towards the beach. Come on, we can go in now.'

Cautiously, Wendy followed Meg into the coffee shop. As they seated themselves, she glanced out of the window and could see Burke Flint as he sauntered slowly away. She sighed deeply with relief, and turned to Meg.

'I'm sorry, Meg,' she grimaced, feeling like a fool now that it was over. 'It was such a shock seeing him like that. I almost walked inside.'

Meg eyed her curiously from across the table. 'You know,' she said slowly, 'I don't know what you're so afraid of. Surely he's forgotten that scene you had in the dining room, the water you spilled on him. He won't attack you, for heaven's sake.'

'You don't understand,' Wendy said. 'It's not just that.' She toyed nervously with her napkin.

Meg watched her appraisingly for several moments, then stated flatly, 'There's more to it, then, this phobia you have about Burke Flint.' Wendy nodded, staring down at the paper napkin which was now in shreds on the table.

'Yes,' she said dully. 'There's more.'

'But you don't want to talk about it.'

'I'd really rather not,' Wendy said, meeting her

friend's eyes. 'It's not that I don't trust you,' she said quickly, noting the hurt look in Meg's eyes. 'I just want to forget about it and stay out of his way.' She put her elbows on the table and cupped her chin in her hands, staring miserably out of the window. 'I was crazy to stay here,' she said. 'I should have known I'd have to run into him sooner or later.'

Meg snorted. 'Crazy, my eye! It was the smartest thing you ever did. Have you looked in a mirror lately? When I first met you on the plane, you were a pitiful sight. Even with all my problems, I felt sorry for you. Now you look like a million dollars. You've put on a little weight in the right places, you've got a terrific tan, you laugh and smile once in a while, and you like your work. That doesn't sound so crazy to me.'

Wendy had to smile. Meg was right. She was being silly, paranoid. She did feel like a different person and knew she looked better. Actually, she thought in some surprise, I'm happy—and strong enough to keep from making a fool of myself over Burke Flint.

'You're right, of course,' she said. She gave Meg's hand a squeeze. 'Thanks, friend.'

'Think nothing of it,' Meg said gruffly. 'Now, can we please order some lunch? I'm starving.'

These FOUR free Harlequin Romance novels allow you to enter the world of romance, love and desire. As a member of the Harlequin Home Subscription Plan, you can continue to experience all the moods of love. You'll be inspired by moments so real. . .so moving. . .you won't want them to end. So start your own Harlequin Romance adventure by returning the reply card below. <u>DO IT TODAY!</u>

EXTRA BONUS
MAIL YOUR ORDER
TODAY AND GET A
FREE TOTE BAG
FROM HARLEQUIN.

CHAPTER FIVE

By the next day Wendy was feeling decidedly foolish about her panic at seeing Burke Flint in the
coffee shop. After all, she reasoned as she sat at her
desk typing up his tapes, what in the world can he
do to me? I'm a grown woman. I feel stronger than I
have in weeks. He can't force me to do anything I
don't want to do, so what difference does it make
even if he does see me?

'Do you have any more of this draft paper?' she
called to Meg across the expanse of the two desks.
'I've just used my last piece.'

'Supplies are in Mr Patera's office,' Meg
answered. She was deeply involved in a numerical
chart that was about to drive her crazy. 'In the
cupboard opposite his desk.'

Wendy got up and went into Mr Patera's office.
He was off on his morning rounds, and the office
was empty. She found the cupboard and was rum-
maging around looking for the kind of paper she
had been using on Burke Flint's book when she
heard voices coming from the other room.

It wasn't unheard of for guests who wanted typing done by the hotel staff to come to the office, but
it was unusual. Most of them preferred to send their
work with a waiter and discuss it over the telephone, possibly in the belief that an actual appearance in the office destroyed the illusion that they
were supposed to be on a vacation.

Wendy found the draft paper she was looking for, gathered up a stack of it and started back into her office, curious to see who it was Meg was talking to. She had already stepped into the room when she saw him and caught his swift glance and look of dawning recognition. She thought later that she must have known unconsciously that it was Burke Flint's voice she had heard, that before she saw him a part of her knew who it was.

Still, it gave her such a jolt to find herself looking into those grey eyes, that stern face, that she was momentarily speechless.

He was at her desk, one hip resting on the edge. When he saw her in the doorway, his eyes widened at first in disbelief, and he slowly rose to his full height, the eyes narrowing now, sparks flying from them. Wendy glanced briefly at Meg, who stood paralysed at her own desk, her face red.

Wendy stood stock-still, clutching the stack of papers in her hands and gazing from one to the other. Burke stared at her, his eyes accusing.

'Uh,' Meg began, 'Wendy, Mr Flint just stopped by to congratulate me on my improved spelling.'

Against her will, Wendy's eyes fastened on Burke's steely gaze. She was mesmerised by that icy glare. Meg's explanations rambled on, but neither of them heard a word, their eyes locked together. Finally, Meg's voice trailed off weakly and there was silence in the small room.

Then he spoke. 'Where in the hell have you been?' he ground out through clenched teeth.

The electricity in the air was so thick it was almost palpable, as though a spark could set off a conflagration at any time. Dimly, through her daze,

Wendy heard Meg's chair scrape as she pushed it back from her desk, heard her mumble an excuse lamely, and scurry out of the room.

'Well?' Burke shouted when Meg was gone, the door softly closed behind her.

He took a step towards her. Wendy gave a little cry and instinctively stepped back. He made an angry sound deep in his throat and gave her a disgusted look.

'For God's sake, I'm not going to attack you,' he said.

He glanced down at her typewriter where she had left a half-finished page of his manuscript before she had gone in search of more paper. He read in silence for a moment, then slowly raised his eyes to meet hers.

'I see now why the spelling has improved so dramatically,' he said flatly.

He gave her an inquiring look, but still she could only shrink back from him. Her head was spinning, and she couldn't think straight. She found him overpoweringly attractive, felt drawn to him almost irresistibly, yet the shock of seeing him there in the office, and a lingering fear of him, left her limp and confused.

Some inkling of her state of mind must have finally got through to him. As he stood gazing at her, trembling before him, his eyes softened and his mouth began to twitch humorously. He spread his hands wide, and Wendy caught her breath when she saw how the gesture tightened the white-knit shirt across the broad shoulders and strong arm muscles.

'You know,' he said slowly, 'your obvious fear

only incites my lust.' He grinned. 'So for the sake of your virginal purity you'd better try to get yourself under control.'

She couldn't help smiling at that, and gradually the tension began to ebb out of her. She started across the room towards her desk, keenly aware as she did so that his eyes followed her, every step of the way.

Since for the most part Wendy and Meg worked alone in the office, they dressed casually on the job. Today Wendy had on a pale blue dirndl skirt, cinched in at the waist with a blue and white straw belt, and a white cotton blouse with a round elasticised neckline.

Without vanity, she was well aware of the fact that she had picked up most of the weight she had lost, that her skin bloomed once again with health, and that her long dark hair, in the loose knot at the back of her neck, shone with vitality.

Very carefully she skirted around the tall figure, and when the desk was safely between them, she set down the stack of paper and looked at him.

He put the palms of his hands down flat on the desk and leaned towards her over it, so that his face was only a foot away from hers. She resisted the impulse to step back, and stood her ground, waiting, willing herself to remain calm.

'I've looked everywhere for you,' he said finally. 'When I inquired at the hotel desk and they said you'd checked out, I couldn't believe it.'

He reached out a hand, but at the look of alarm in her eyes, he stopped before he actually touched her, and dropped it to the top of the desk once more.

'Do I really frighten you that much?' he asked softly, trying to hold her gaze.

She looked away and began straightening the papers on her already neat desk.

'Of course not,' she said briskly. 'As you said, you're not going to attack me.'

'Then why did you vanish like that?'

'I didn't "vanish",' she retorted. 'I simply ran out of money and decided it was time to leave, to get back to my job. Then Meg told me about the opening here at the hotel for a typist and I decided to take it.'

'Without bothering to let me know,' he said grimly. 'Didn't it occur to you that I'd wonder about you?'

She eyed him steadily, feeling stronger now that she was over the initial shock of seeing him again. 'No,' she replied, 'not really.'

'Not even after what happened beween us that night?' His voice was both angry and incredulous.

'No. Why should it? It was just a passing fancy, wasn't it?' she asked lightly. 'It had no meaning for either of us. I told you that night I didn't want to get in over my head.'

'Just what does that mean?' he asked sarcastically. 'I don't recall having forced myself on you that night.'

Wendy bit her lip and turned her head away. For a moment she was tempted to tell him about her experience with David, to explain what it was that she found so frightening about him, that it wasn't what he would do that worried her, but her own fatal weakness. But what would he think of her if he found out she'd been involved with a married man?

'No,' she said finally in a low voice. 'You didn't force yourself on me.'

She heard him draw in his breath sharply. 'Don't do that,' he growled.

She glanced up at him, startled. 'Don't do what?'

'Look so damned forlorn. I warned you what that did to me.'

In a second, he had skirted around the desk, and before she could move he had one hand on her upper arm, the other on her neck, tilting her head back so that she had to look up at him.

'I told you I wouldn't rush you,' he murmured. 'Don't be frightened.'

He bent his head and brushed his lips lightly against hers. Wendy's heart gave a great leap, and a warm glow suffused her whole body. His hand on her arm tightened as he pulled her close to him, and with a sigh she leaned against him, her mouth relaxing and softening under his.

Gently, his lips played against hers, at one moment barely touching, at the next moving sensuously over her whole mouth. He seemed to be holding himself in check, never probing, never insistent, yet the tantalising touch of that soft mouth on hers, the hint of the tip of his tongue, made her faint with pleasurable sensation.

She reached out her hands to steady herself and the contact with the hard muscles of his chest under the thin knit cloth of his shirt only made her head whirl faster.

His hand was moving now, on her neck, slowly, as though his fingers were trying to memorise the contours of her chin, her jaw, her cheeks, then over the little hollow at the base of her throat, her shoulders and upper chest.

As his hand passed slowly and lightly across the neckline of her low-cut blouse, touching lightly on her breast, his kiss deepened, and she knew as she responded to it that once again she was lost.

She felt his hand slip under the elastic top of her blouse to trace the swelling outline of her upper breast, but then, abruptly, he clamped both hands firmly on her shoulders and pushed her away so that their bodies were no longer touching.

She looked up at him. His head was turned slightly away, his eyes hooded, and his breathing harsh as he struggled for control.

Finally, he looked down at her, his mouth quirked in a rueful smile. He removed his hands from her shoulders and stepped back a pace.

'You see,' he said. 'You have nothing to fear from me.'

No, she thought, with an ache in her heart. But what am I going to do about myself? She was more shaken than she could have believed by this sudden encounter. She had had no time to prepare for it mentally. Her pulses were still racing, her face flushed.

She watched him as he backed slowly away from her, his eyes still fastened on hers, a gently mocking smile on his lips.

'Don't look so damned woebegone,' he said with a curt little laugh. He turned and started towards the door. When he reached it he turned around, still smiling. 'And remember, Wendy, it's cottage number eight—just in case.'

After he had gone, Wendy almost fell into her

chair. She felt as though she had been through a violent ordeal, an accident of some kind, from which she had barely escaped with her life. Yet, she thought, what really had happened? A kiss, a brief conversation, nothing more. It seemed as though her whole world had been transformed.

There was a sound of footsteps behind her. Wendy whirled around in her chair, half fearing and half hoping that Burke had come back. When she saw Meg creeping warily into the room, she had to smile.

'It's all right, Meg,' she said. 'He's gone.'

With her eyes glued on Wendy, Meg walked across the room to her own desk and sat down. She rested her elbows on her typewriter and gazed meaningfully at her friend. Her eyes appeared to be bulging out of their sockets, and her mouth hung open.

'Well,' she said finally, 'what was that all about?'

'Oh, nothing,' Wendy replied airily, barely able to suppress the laughter that threatened at the sight of her goggle-eyed friend.

Maliciously, she switched on her cassette-player, put on her earphones, and began to roll a fresh sheet of paper into her typewriter.

'Oh, come on,' Meg wailed. 'You can't do this to me. Wendy,' she commanded, 'stop that and look at me!'

Making a fruitless and feeble attempt to keep a straight face, Wendy finally broke down into helpless laughter. She pulled of her earphones and turned to Meg.

'All right,' she said, 'I'm looking.'

'What happened?' Meg pleaded. 'I can't stand it.

What's going on between you and Burke Flint? It's got to be more than just a glass of water in his lap. The look on his face when you came into the room just now was enough to kill.'

'Well, yes,' Wendy admitted, sighing, 'you could say that.'

'Well?' Meg said. 'Are you going to tell me?'

'Would it do any good to say I'd rather not?' Wendy asked. But when she saw the stricken look on Meg's face, she realised she couldn't do that, not after Meg had witnessed so much of the recent scene between Wendy and Burke Flint.

'Well,' she began, 'he did buy me a drink one night.'

Meg's eyes widened. 'And?'

Wendy shrugged. 'We talked. We danced.' Her voice trailed off. She didn't want to go into details about the romantic ending to that evening later, in the garden.

'Is that all?' Meg asked.

'Well, just about.'

'I see,' Meg said flatly, 'and on the basis of one drink, a little conversation, a dance, you decide to cut your vacation short and go back to Baltimore, go into a panic at the thought of Burke Flint even seeing you, and he just about has a stroke when he finds you working here.'

Wendy smiled weakly. 'Put that way it does sound a little feeble,' she admitted. She had no intention, however, of spelling out any details. 'Let's just say that what actually happened was more than I'm telling and less than what you're thinking.'

Meg sighed deeply. 'Okay, okay. I get the picture. Although why you're trying to escape from a man like that . . . Unless, that is, he tried to rape you. Even then, I don't know how much resistance I'd put up.'

'Meg!' Wendy exclaimed. 'Of course he didn't try to rape me. He wouldn't do a thing like that. He's not that kind of man.'

Meg only shook her head and turned to her work. 'I still don't get it,' she muttered.

Wendy didn't blame her for her bewilderment. She felt totally confused herself. She knew the only thing she was afraid of was her own reaction to that formidably attractive man.

She wondered why he did continue to pursue her, why he had been so angry when she disappeared. It could have been mere vanity. A man like Burke Flint certainly couldn't be accustomed to women fleeing his advances.

In that case, she thought as she slowly put her earphones back on, the situation was even more dangerous. He wouldn't let up until he'd won, until he'd broken through her defences and made her submit.

She shuddered at that. She had to admit that she was powerfully attracted to him, not only physically, but as a person. She also, grudgingly, carrying it a step further, had to admit that she would probably enjoy very much going to bed with him. To deny that would be a bald lie.

But what about love? What about commitment?

For the next few days Wendy tried to put all thoughts of Burke Flint out of her mind. The tapes continued to flow into the office, and she found herself becoming more and more intrigued with the story.

She guessed that the book was about half finished and wondered vaguely what would happen when it was finally completed. Would he leave Nassau then? Go off on another assignment to a different part of the world?

She couldn't help comparing their lives, his so exciting and sophisticated, hers so mundane and humdrum, so ordinary. Yes, she thought—and safe. She wasn't made for adventure. The episode with David was enough excitement to last a lifetime for her.

During those two days after Burke's dramatic appearance in the office, Wendy hadn't even caught a glimpse of him around the hotel. She kept expecting to run into him, constantly on guard for his pursuit, but nothing at all happened. She was both relieved and a little disappointed. She knew, however, from the steady flow of tapes that he must be working hard on his book.

Then, suddenly, on the third day, the tapes stopped coming. Usually when Wendy arrived at her desk in the morning, there would be a neat pile waiting for her of four to six tapes that Burke had sent up with the waiter. Wendy would type them up, erase the tapes, then send the manuscript pages and tapes back during the afternoon.

This morning there were no tapes at all on her desk. She felt shocked, bereft, as though a friend had gone away, and she realised that she had come to depend on hearing that low confident voice in her ears all day, even to look forward to it.

Just then Meg breezed into the office and hurried over to her desk. She gave Wendy an apologetic look.

'Sorry I'm late. I overslept again,' she mumbled.

'Oh, that's okay,' Wendy said. 'No problem.'

In fact, Meg's tardiness had become habitual for the past few days. Wendy didn't mind. She was quite satisfied with their system of dividing the work, where she did Burke's tapes and Meg took on all the other odds and ends that came into the office from the other guests. Besides, Meg always stayed to finish her work in the afternoon.

Still, something about her friend's manner bothered Wendy, and she gave her a sharp look.

Meg was concentrating hard on removing the cover of her typewriter, her eyes straight ahead. Her face was unnaturally flushed, and she was biting her lip.

'Meg,' Wendy began slowly, 'is something wrong?'

Meg darted a quick look at her and gave a weak smile.

'Wrong? What could be wrong?'

'That's what I'm asking you,' Wendy said drily. 'Look, you do more than your share of work around here, and for all I care you can come in at midnight and work until eight in the morning. It's just that you've been acting funny lately, and if you've got a problem, I'd like to help if I can.'

Meg flushed a darker shade of red and began rolling the platen of her typewriter back and forth idly. She seemed to be deep in thought, and Wendy waited in silence.

Finally, Meg got up and began pacing about the room. Wendy watched her, wondering if she should force her to speak or just leave it alone. Meg stopped her pacing at last and stood at her desk, frowning. Then she looked at Wendy and sighed.

'It's Ken,' she announced.

'Ken?' Wendy asked blankly. 'Ken who?' She wondered if Meg's husband had contacted her in some way.

Meg made an impatient gesture with her hand. 'You know. Ken Harris. The desk clerk.' Once again she flushed a deep red.

Suddenly the light dawned on Wendy. Apparently Meg was trying to tell her that she had some kind of interest in Ken Harris. Given her romantic nature, Wendy could guess what kind of interest.

'I see,' she said, stalling for time.

She knew Ken Harris, of course, or at least knew who he was—a quiet, sandy-haired young man who worked at the front desk on the day shift. He seemed pleasant enough, nice-looking. Wendy, preoccupied with her own problems, hadn't given him much thought one way or the other.

How selfish I've been, she thought, so absorbed in David and then in Burke Flint, I haven't even considered Meg and her problems.

'Sit down, Meg,' she said gently, 'and tell me about it.'

Meg gave her a look of relief. 'Are you sure?' she asked.

'Sure I'm sure,' Wendy replied briskly, more ashamed of herself than ever at her thoughtlessness. 'Come on, sit down.'

Meg plopped herself down in her chair and turned eagerly to Wendy. The troubled look disappeared as the words came tumbling out in a torrent.

'I noticed him right away,' she said excitedly, 'as

soon as I walked in that first day and saw him behind the desk. Wendy, I've always loved those strong silent types. Then later, when I got to know him better and saw how kind and gentle he was, I just flipped.' She was grinning broadly by now. 'He's considerate and thoughtful, and . . .' Her voice trailed off and the worried look reappeared.

'Well,' Wendy said, 'so what's the problem?'

'The problem is,' Meg said, staring out of the window, 'that I'm scared to death.'

Wendy laughed shortly. 'I can identify with that sentiment,' she said with feeling. 'Once burned, twice shy. Is that what you mean?'

'Oh, yes,' Meg sighed. 'That's exactly what I mean. What am I going to do?'

Wendy thought hard for a moment. Since she was terrified out of her wits by Burke Flint and what that relationship might cost her, she was probably the last person to advise Meg. Still, she thought, she had to give it a try.

'Well,' she began slowly, 'how do things stand now?'

Meg shrugged. 'We've talked a lot together, you know, taken walks, had a drink or two. He knows about my marriage and divorce. He's so high-minded himself that he got really angry when I told him what had happened.' She hesitated. 'It was then that I realised he was interested in me, you know, as a woman.'

Wendy had listened carefully to Meg's story, giving it all her attention. 'I still don't see what the problem is,' she said. 'Is he forcing any issues?'

'You mean, trying to get me into bed?' She thought a minute. 'No, I don't think so. That is, I think he'd *like* to, but he's not the kind to push. He's not one of these arrogant, over-confident types.'

Not like Burke Flint, Wendy thought wryly, who seemed to corner her into a threatening confrontation every time they met.

'Then what exactly is it you're afraid of?' Wendy asked quietly. 'It sounds to me as though you're darned lucky to have such a nice man interested in you.'

Meg wrung her hands and screwed up her face. 'I don't *know*,' she wailed. 'That's just the trouble.' She got up and started pacing again. 'I like him, I really like him a lot. And I know he likes me.'

'Well, then?' Wendy asked.

Meg stopped short. Her eyes widened. As she stared at Wendy, she seemed visibly to relax.

'You're right,' she said with wonder in her voice. 'Oh, thank you, Wendy.'

'What did I say?' Wendy asked with a little laugh.

'It isn't what you said,' Meg replied, 'but you listened. That's all it takes sometimes.' She sat down at her desk and rolled a fresh sheet of paper into her typewriter. 'I see now that I've put it into words just how silly I was being.' She shook her head. 'Holding things in only makes them *loom* and seem much worse than they really are.'

'Well, I'm glad you feel better. Not so scared any more?'

'No, not now that I see there's nothing to be afraid of.'

'What were you afraid of?' Wendy asked.

Meg gave her a direct look. 'The same thing you are—getting hurt again.'

Wendy flushed. 'I see. And now suddenly you don't think you will get hurt?'

'Oh, no,' Meg replied, widening her eyes. 'There's always that risk. I only see that if I insist on playing it safe—with Ken or anyone else—I could miss out on any chance of happiness at all.'

Wendy sighed. 'You're probably right. But it's not easy.'

'No,' Meg said with a shrug. 'I don't guess anything worthwhile ever is.' She switched on her tape recorder. 'Well, better get to work, now that we've solved the problems of the world.' She glanced at Wendy's bare, neat desk. 'Say, where is your morning supply of tapes?'

'I was wondering that myself,' Wendy replied. 'Maybe our Mr Flint is giving himself a little vacation—or maybe the creative well of genius has run dry.'

Meg snorted and began sorting through the pile of folders on her desk. 'Some vacation!' she said. 'Wait'll you get a look at the blonde who moved into his cottage this morning.'

Wendy's heart stopped. She felt as though someone had just punched her hard in the stomach. Quickly, she composed her face and said in a careful voice, 'What blonde is that?'

Meg had started typing. 'Oh, one of those expensive ones. You know, not cheap or vulgar, very discreetly sexy and high-class.'

Of course, Wendy thought bitterly, Burke Flint would only want the very best.

'Did you see her?' Wendy asked, trying to sound offhand.

'Just a glimpse this morning on my way to work,'

Meg said over the clatter of the typewriter. 'She was at the front desk when I stopped by to talk to Ken.' She laughed. 'For a minute there I was worried about Ken. She's really something, and I was relieved, I can tell you, when Ken told me she was Mr Flint's guest. It's a good thing . . .'

Suddenly she stopped typing and with a look of horror on her face turned to Wendy, clapping a hand over her open mouth.

'Oh lord, Wendy,' she muttered, aghast. 'Me and my big mouth.'

'It's okay,' Wendy said quickly, forcing out a smile. 'I told you I didn't want to have anything more to do with Burke Flint.'

'Well,' Meg said hesitantly, 'you did say that.'

'That's right,' Wendy said, more firmly now that she had recovered from the initial shock, 'and I meant it. This blonde visitor of his only proves how right I was.'

Meg still looked troubled. 'Listen,' she said, 'Ken has a friend who works at the Seacliff Hotel down the way. Maybe we could all get together and do something some night.'

Wendy held up a hand and smiled. 'No thanks, Meg. I appreciate the thought, but when I said no entanglements, I meant it. Besides, I think you and Ken need to be alone for now until you find out where you're going.'

'Well,' Meg said, 'if you're sure.'

'I'm sure,' Wendy stated flatly. 'Now, since I'm out of a job until Mr Flint gets his act together and starts working on his book again, how about sharing some of your work with me.'

*

The next few days were lonely and empty ones for Wendy. She missed working on Burke's book more than she would have thought possible. Meg was so taken up with Ken Harris that Wendy hardly saw her at all outside the office.

In a way, though, she enjoyed this time alone. She became deeply involved in Burke's book on Vietnam, took long walks by herself, wrote letters to Greta and her other friends in Baltimore and enjoyed swimming around the little coves of the island.

She had seen nothing at all of Burke Flint and his blonde guest. Since hotel employees and guests were not encouraged to fraternise, this was understandable. Wendy so far had managed to push thoughts of that disturbing man out of her mind whenever they arose, and the presence in his life of another woman helped tremendously.

One day, right before five o'clock, Meg pushed her chair back away from her desk with a deep sigh and a groan of weariness. There had been a convention of American Bar Association lawyers at the hotel during the past week, and even without Burke Flint's tapes, the two girls had been rushed off their feet trying to keep up with the increased flow of work.

Meg stood up, yawned hugely and stretched her arms above her head.

'I am beat!' she exclaimed. 'Thank goodness this is their last day here.'

Wendy smiled. 'Amen,' she said. 'I thought they were supposed to be a convention. They might as well all be back in their offices.'

She looked up to find Meg staring at her, a thoughtful look on her face.

'What are you going to do tonight?' she asked finally.

Wendy shrugged. 'Oh, the usual. Maybe go for a swim, read, do a little laundry.'

'Sounds thrilling,' Meg remarked drily as she covered her typewriter. She put her hands on her hips and glared. 'Haven't you had enough yet?'

Wendy was puzzled. 'I don't follow you. Enough what?'

'Enough of your own company, that's what!' Meg spluttered. 'Honestly, I thought if I just left you alone for a while you'd decide to take me up on my offer, but I see I'm going to have to push.'

'What offer?' Wendy asked in a bewildered tone. 'I don't have the faintest idea what you're talking about.'

Meg marched around the desks and planted herself squarely in front of Wendy, an exasperated look on her face.

'What offer! I told you a few days ago that Ken had a friend who wanted to meet you. You were so cool to the idea that I figured you were carrying a torch for Burke Flint.'

Wendy's eyes widened. 'You never said anything about anyone wanting to meet me,' she said.

Meg coloured. 'Well, I might have left that part out.'

Wendy had to smile. 'That's a pretty important part.'

'Well, anyway,' Meg brushed her aside, 'his name is John Frazier. He's tall and blond and tan and looks like Robert Redford. He would like to meet you, and he is *not* married, and I said I would produce you for dinner tonight.'

Meg glared defiantly, anticipating in advance the objections that were already forming in Wendy's mind. Wendy stared back, and the thought arose, Why not? She *was* getting bored with her own company.

'Okay,' she said. 'Why not?'

'Do you mean it?' Meg asked, stunned.

'Sure.'

'Well, come on, quick, let's go get ready before you change your mind.'

Wendy found herself humming as she showered and dressed. She was looking forward to a night out, to some pleasant company.

She decided to wear her black cotton dress with the tiny straps and low-cut bodice. She hadn't worn it since that night—it seemed ages ago—that the air-conditioning went off and she had had a drink in the lounge with Burke Flint.

She stood still in front of her dresser mirror, remembering how they had talked and danced, then, later, out in the garden, his arms around her, holding her close, his mouth on hers, his hands caressing her . . .

'No,' she said out loud. Her whole body was trembling, on fire. She reached out a hand on the dresser to steady herself. 'No,' she whispered. 'I will not let myself think about it. It was nothing.'

Gradually, her breathing returned to normal, the trembling ceased, and she could smile at her reflection. She zipped up the dress, which fit her perfectly again now that she had gained her weight back, and began vigorously to brush her long, silky dark hair

It really was nothing, she repeated to herself as

she brushed. We both got a little carried away. It was silly of me ever to try to avoid him. And that day in the office, he was just taken by surprise to see me because he'd thought I'd gone.

She decided to wear her hair loose that night. It fell in soft, sleek waves about her face down to her shoulders. She put on a dab of pale lipstick and a touch of eye make-up. With her golden tan, that's all she needed.

There was a light knock on the door. She opened it, and Meg walked in, wearing a bright yellow sheath.

'Don't tell me you haven't changed your mind,' she commented sarcastically. 'I can't believe it.'

'Oh, come on, Meg, let's forget about that. I'm ready to enjoy myself.'

'Good. Ken will drive us over to the Seacliff. John works there. He manages the restaurant. We'll meet him there.'

'Sounds good to me. Let's go.' Wendy picked up her white stole and draped it casually around her shoulders.

Ken Harris was waiting for them at the front desk. Wendy knew him, of course, since they both worked in the same hotel. He was built like an athlete, not tall, but muscular, with sandy hair and kind hazel eyes.

'I can't believe it,' he remarked as the two girls walked towards him. 'Two women—two gorgeous women—and both on time.'

Meg frowned and poked him in the ribs with her elbow as she passed by. 'Very funny, Mr Harris,' she remarked.

'How are you, Ken?' Wendy asked. She suddenly felt very nervous. It had been so long since she'd been out on a real date—a blind date, at that. She began to regret the impulse that had moved her to agree to come.

As if she could read her friend's thoughts, Meg gripped her tightly by the arm. 'You're not going to back out now, my friend,' she muttered under her breath.

'Why, Meg,' Wendy replied innocently, 'how could you think I would do such a thing?'

Meg only snorted, but did relax her hold on Wendy's arm.

The Seacliff Hotel was only a mile or so down the beach from the Emerald Beach, but up much higher, on a sort of promontory that overlooked the sea, and, across the cove, the small city of Nassau with its sparkling lights.

The restaurant was set out on the edge of the cliff, cantilevered for support, so that one had the illusion of sitting in some sort of airborne vehicle suspended over the sea. Even the ceiling was glass, with stars and moon shining down on them.

John Frazier was at the entrance to the restaurant to greet them.

'John,' Ken was saying, 'this is Wendy Fuller.' There was a note of pride in his voice, Wendy noticed, as though he was presenting his friend with some kind of prize animal.

'How do you do,' Wendy said, a little embarrassed by the direct stare John was giving her from startlingly blue eyes.

'So this is the famous Wendy,' he murmured in her ear as he took her by the elbow and deftly guided her across the crowded room.

Oh, oh, Wendy thought to herself, not another smooth operator. She sighed and hoped she wouldn't have to beat him off before the evening was over.

Their table was one of the best in the room, by the windows overlooking the breathtaking view. They settled themselves on the curved banquette, John and Wendy on one side, Ken and Meg on the other.

Over drinks the conversation was general and impersonal, all four entering in. They talked about their jobs, their homes in the States. Wendy was from Baltimore, Meg from Phoenix, Ken from New York, and John from California.

Gradually, however, after the second round of drinks, Wendy noticed that Ken and Meg had moved closer together. Their conversation became more personal and finally was directed only at each other.

There was a muted steel band playing softly in the background, the service was excellent, and with the help of two sherries, Wendy began to relax and enjoy herself.

'Meg tells me you manage the restaurant here, John,' she said. 'You must do a fine job because it certainly seems to be running smoothly.'

'Thank you. I love it,' he said simply.

'That's probably the key to doing a good job, wouldn't you say? To love what you're doing?' she asked.

'Absolutely. How about you? Are you enjoying your job at the Emerald Beach?'

She thought for a moment. 'It's very pleasant,

and the work is interesting, but I'm afraid I'm not very career-oriented.'

He laughed. 'I see. An old-fashioned girl.'

'You find that funny?' she asked, a little annoyed.

'Not at all,' he hastened to assure her. 'I find it a little unusual these days—but nice.' He smiled at her. 'Very nice.'

She returned his smile. 'That's all right, then,' she said.

'Would you care to dance?'

She nodded her assent, and they got up and walked out on to the small dance floor. Just as he reached for her, smiling, she saw, over his shoulder, the tall form of Burke Flint just entering the room, a slender blonde hanging on to his arm.

Wendy closed her eyes and gave a barely audible gasp, swaying slightly. It was such a shock to see him here so unexpectedly.

'Are you okay?' John asked with concern. He took hold of her arms to steady her.

She opened her eyes. Burke was gone. 'Yes,' she said, forcing a smile. 'Of course. It was just the wine. I'm a poor drinker.'

He grinned at her, showing even, very white teeth against his deeply tanned face, and pulled her gently into his arms.

They danced silently, giving Wendy a chance to recover herself. What a fool I am, she thought, to go to pieces every time I see that man. Never again, she promised herself.

The next thing she knew, Burke Flint had tapped a startled John on the shoulder, murmuring 'May I?', and she was in his arms.

CHAPTER SIX

WENDY'S first sensation on finding herself propelled smoothly about the dance floor in the arms of Burke Flint was of sheer, heavenly joy. For just a few seconds she closed her eyes and gave herself up mindlessly to that exquisite pleasure.

In a moment, however, she came to her senses. Her eyes flew open and she looked up to see those hard grey eyes fastened on her, a quirky smile, smug, self-satisfied, on the thin lips.

'Just what do you think you're doing?' she cried, stopping in the middle of the dance floor and removing her hand from around his neck.

'Shh,' he said under his breath, his grin broadening. 'Do you want to create a public scene?'

He pulled her closer. Her body went rigid and she tried to pull her other hand free from his grasp. Over his shoulder she could see John Frazier standing at the edge of the dance floor staring after them as they moved farther away, a puzzled frown on his handsome face.

'You really are insufferable,' Wendy spluttered as she feebly tried to release herself from that iron grip. 'You're rude, arrogant and . . .'

'I like you, too,' he said with a little laugh, and tightened his hold on her.

Wendy knew when she was beaten. He realised she wouldn't create a scene. He was enjoying himself immensely, and she decided the only thing she could do was to relax and wait for an opportunity to escape, or hope John would come to her rescue.

The trouble was, she thought with mounting dismay, as she relaxed and lay passive in his arms she was becoming more intensely aware of his sheer, overpowering physical presence and the effect it was having on her, the way his large strong hand held hers, the masculine scent of his smooth dark jacket, the way his arm encircled her small waist possessively, the fingers gently kneading caressing.

The next thing she knew they had danced out on to a large, open-air deck. There were a few other couples out there, and the music from the dining room drifted out through the open french doors.

He was humming softly, off-key, as he guided her firmly over to a secluded corner. There he stopped, put his hands on her shoulders and stood looking down at her gravely, his eyes dark in the shadows, piercing into hers.

Gathering up all her strength, Wendy tried to slither out of his grasp, but his grip was firm. She could see him grinning.

'Just what do you think you're doing?' she said in a low angry tone. 'Let me go.'

His dark heavy eyebrows shot up. 'Is that really what you want?' he asked in a mocking tone.

'It certainly is,' she said firmly.

He released her so suddenly that she almost lost her balance. Recovering herself at last, realising she was free, she turned quickly to go.

'Not so fast,' he said, and clamped his hand on her bare arm, pulling her around to face him.

He bent his head. She watched, mesmerised

knowing what was coming, but unable to move a muscle. The moment his lips met hers, a shaft of fire pierced her heart. His mouth moved softly, teasingly on hers. Her head began to spin and she felt her lips part slowly, and she closed her eyes.

Then, suddenly, Burke lifted his head. She looked up at him, puzzled. His eyes were glittering in the dimness.

'Yes,' he said huskily, 'that's what I wanted.'

'What did you want?'

'To find out.'

'To find out what?' she murmured, transfixed by those eyes.

He didn't answer. Instead, he took her lightly in his arms, holding her at a distance, and danced her back into the dining room.

'Where are we going?' she asked, in a daze. He had started humming again.

'I'm taking you back to your young man,' he said in a matter-of-fact tone.

Just like that, she thought. She began to grow angry. He had made a fool of her again.

'And back to your young lady,' she remarked nastily.

'Well, yes, you could put it that way,' he said lightly. 'Jealous?'

They were just inside the door now. Wendy stopped short and pulled back, glaring at him.

'Jealous!' she exclaimed. 'Listen, Mr Wonderful, all I want from you is to be left alone. I've told you that repeatedly, but you can't seem to understand. I am not the least bit interested in your advances. I don't know why you insist on forcing yourself on me.'

'Oh, really?' he inquired innocently. 'Somehow I don't get that impression. You seemed quite interested a moment ago.'

Wendy was so angry now that she didn't trust herself to speak. She simply whirled around and stalked off. Somehow she knew that as she moved away from him he was looking after her with that same mocking, hard-eyed grin.

As she made her way back to her table to join the others, she saw John coming towards her, frowning.

'I was just coming to look for you,' he said, taking her by the arm. 'What was that all about?'

'It's nothing,' she said. 'Nothing at all. A mistake.'

They started walking towards the table. Wendy knew John was annoyed, but she didn't care at this point. She wasn't going to make any explanations. She was sick of male egos and arrogant demanding men.

'Look,' he said stiffly, 'I'm sorry. I didn't mean to butt in. I just thought you might need some help.'

Wendy was instantly contrite. Here was this perfectly nice, innocent man, just trying to show her a pleasant evening, and she was letting Burke Flint spoil it.

She put a hand on John's arm and looked up into his troubled blue eyes.

'No,' she said softly. 'I'm the one who's sorry. It really was nothing. Just some unfinished business I had to take care of.'

'I see,' he said dubiously. He thought for a moment. 'And is it finished now?'

'Definitely,' she said, forcing a grin.

John's tense face relaxed into a pleasant boy-ish smile. 'That's good,' he said. 'Are you hungry?'

'Starved.'

'Well, come on, then, let's go.'

They got home late that night, and the next morning both girls were bleary-eyed at their desks. Luckily, the lawyers had gone home, there were still no tapes from Burke Flint, and there was very little work to do.

'Did you have a good time last night?' Meg asked over coffee in the middle of the morning.

'Yes, I did,' Wendy replied. She smiled at Meg's dubious look. 'I really did.'

She had, too, she thought, once she had banished the little episode with Burke from her mind. Apparently he and his blonde friend had left right afterwards, because she hadn't seen them again all evening.

'How did you like John?'

'Oh, very much,' Wendy replied truthfully. 'He's so nice, and such good company.'

John Frazier was one of those handsome men remarkably unconscious of their own good looks. After the air had been cleared over her short disappearance with Burke Flint, John had really put himself out to show her a pleasant evening.

'Are you going to see him again?'

'Well, he did say something about a party a friend of his was giving, next weekend, I think.'

'Maybe we could do something together,' Meg said. 'I mean the four of us.'

'That would be nice,' Wendy replied. She smiled. 'Although I get the impression you and Ken would prefer to be alone.'

Meg coloured violently and set her coffee cup down on her desk. 'Well,' she mumbled, 'not all the time.' She glanced shyly at Wendy. 'Do you like him? Ken, I mean.'

'Yes, very much,' Wendy replied. 'I think he's just right for you.'

The quiet, sandy-haired Ken was a perfect foil for the vivacious redhead, Wendy thought. He had just sat and beamed protectively, admiringly at her all evening.

Meg sighed. 'I think so, too. It's almost too good to be true.'

'Do you think it's serious?' Wendy asked.

Meg shrugged. 'Who knows? I think it could be. But we both want to give it some time.'

'I think that's wise,' Wendy agreed.

Meg sipped her coffee in silence for a while, idly inspecting the folders on her desk. Then she turned to Wendy.

'What was that all about with Burke Flint last night?' she asked.

'It was nothing,' Wendy replied shortly. 'A misunderstanding.'

'Oh, come on, now,' Meg objected. 'A week ago he came barging in here with fire in his eyes when he saw you, then last night he spirits you off in a corner for half an hour, and you tell me it was nothing!'

'It wasn't half an hour,' Wendy exclaimed. 'More like ten minutes.'

Meg giggled. 'If you'd seen the look on that

blonde's face, you would have been dead by now. She was livid.'

'Well, I don't blame her,' Wendy said hotly. 'It was a rude thing to do.'

'What did he want?' Meg asked, bursting with curiosity. 'Why did he do it?'

Wendy sighed. 'To be honest with you, Meg, I really don't know. He thinks he's playing some kind of cat and mouse game with me, but I made it clear last night that I wasn't having any.'

'Did you really?' Meg asked with irony in her voice. 'You looked pretty starry-eyed to me when you emerged from that deck.'

'Oh, Meg, don't be silly. Burke Flint is one of those conceited, overbearing men who thinks every woman is going to fall in a swoon at his feet if he just crooks his little finger. I just have to make it clear to him that I'm not one of them.'

'You think all he wants is to get you in his bed, then?' Meg asked.

'I don't think it,' Wendy retorted, 'I know it.'

'And you're not having any.'

'Of course not,' Wendy exclaimed. 'I'd be a fool to play that game with a man like Burke Flint.'

'Well,' Meg said judiciously, 'I'm not so sure about that.' Her eyes went soft and dreamy. 'What an experience that would be to comfort yourself with in your old age.'

Wendy had to laugh. 'Meg, if I let myself get involved with Burke Flint, I probably wouldn't have an old age to worry about. Come on, now, let's get to work.'

*

The next morning, mysteriously, the tapes from Burke Flint began appearing again.

'Well,' Meg commented, 'I see our genius is back at work.'

'It looks that way,' Wendy said, idly glancing through them. There were only three, about half his usual output.

'That's probably because the blonde left,' Meg said, seating herself at her desk. She started flipping through the stack of folders.

Wendy didn't say anything for a few minutes. Then, 'How do you know she left?' she asked casually.

'Oh, didn't I tell you?' Meg asked innocently. 'Ken said she left right after lunch yesterday.'

Wendy didn't reply. She slipped a tape into the recorder and rolled a fresh sheet of paper into her typewriter. She could feel Meg's eyes following her every movement.

'I guess you're not interested,' Meg finally remarked.

'Not really,' Wendy replied. She put on her earphones and began to type.

Wendy had finished the tapes by the middle of the afternoon. She clipped the draft pages together, slipped a rubber band around the erased tapes, and set both on the tray for the waiter to pick up and return to the cottage.

Meg had left early, right after lunch. It was Friday, their slowest day, and she and Ken were taking the boat over to Miami for the weekend. Ken's parents were down from New York, and he wanted them to meet Meg.

She glanced at her watch. It was three o'clock.

Surely they wouldn't be getting any more work to do today. She felt restless. She wanted to go for a swim or take a walk, play tennis, anything, she thought as she went over to the window and glanced out at the beach.

What's wrong with me, she wondered. Did I make a mistake when I decided to stay here? She would call Greta that night—maybe she should go back to Baltimore. She began to pace the room.

What's wrong with me, she asked herself again. She glanced at the pile of manuscript on the tray and her heart lurched. Oh, no, she wailed silently, it can't be him. She clenched her fists at her sides. I won't let it be him, she thought.

Then she remembered the sound of his voice on the tapes. She recalled thinking at the time, vaguely, how much she had missed hearing it on the days he had been idle.

She had just made up her mind, in desperation, to go into Mr Patera's office to ask if she couldn't leave early, when the connecting door opened and his shiny bald head and worried round face appeared in the doorway.

'Oh, Wendy,' he said with a sigh of relief. 'I'm glad you're still here. One of the guests just called and needs you to go take some dictation.'

'Oh, no,' she said, dismayed.

'What's wrong?' he snapped. 'You do take short-hand, don't you?'

'Well, yes, but . . .' She faltered. 'Well, it's Friday afternoon.'

'I'm aware of that,' he said stiffly. 'Mr Flint's tape recorder is broken, and he needs to get on with his book.'

'Mr Flint?' she asked in a small voice. 'Burke Flint?'

'Yes. Now, you get down to his cottage right away. It's number eight.'

'I'd really rather not,' she hedged. 'Can't he borrow a machine?'

Mr Patera shook his head. 'As a matter of fact I did suggest that, but he seemed to think he'd do better dictating in person than using an unfamiliar machine.'

'Can't he get his fixed?' she asked wildly.

'On Friday afternoon?' he asked incredulously. 'In Nassau? We'll have to send it over to Miami on Monday. In the meantime, you'd better get down there. He's waiting.'

Wendy struggled to fight down the rising panic that threatened to choke her. She could only stare at Mr Patera, one hand at her throat. She sat down limply and leaned over her desk, her head in her hands.

'Are you sick, Wendy?' Mr Patera asked. His tone was stern, but there was a note of concern in his voice.

It was that compassion that brought Wendy to her senses. How could she lie to this kind man? She was behaving childishly, she thought. Gradually, the dreadful pounding in her ears began to recede, and she could breathe normally again.

'No, I'm fine,' she said finally.

She looked up at him and smiled. She was making a fuss about nothing, she thought. It would be good for her to face him, anyway, to get him out of her system once and for all. And if the broken tape recorder was just a ploy to get her down there, she'd soon find out and put a stop to his game. She stood up.

'I'm fine,' she repeated. 'Probably got too much sun yesterday.'

Mr Patera grunted, and Wendy could imagine him muttering to himself inwardly about women and their mysterious problems.

'Well,' he said briskly, 'you'd better get on down there. He sounded quite anxious to get to work. You know how these geniuses are.'

Yes, Wendy thought, only too well. Aloud she said, 'Don't worry. I'll take care of him.'

'Fine. I really appreciate this, Wendy. Don't forget to put in for overtime if you work after five o'clock today or through the weekend.'

He vanished into his office, a self-satisfied smirk on his face. Wendy got a notebook out of her desk drawer and a supply of pencils, newly sharpened. She gathered up the pile of manuscript and the blank tapes, because she might as well deliver them. Then, taking a deep breath, she left.

It wasn't until she was almost at the row of cottages that Wendy realised she was walking on the same brick path through the garden that she and Burke had been on the night the air-conditioning failed.

She had chosen that way because it was cooler, even though the path across the beach was shorter. Now, as she came to the edge of the beach and the stand of palm trees that marked the end of the garden path, she was aware that this was the very spot where he had held her in his arms and where she had so mindlessly responded to him.

For a moment she hesitated. It was so quiet, she

thought. The palms offered scant protection overhead from the burning August sun, but the lush
green vegetation shaded the walk, and the spray of
the sprinklers cooled the air. Only a few scattered
bathers were in the sea, lazing and drifting about in
the striped rubber rafts from the hotel.

It was a beautiful spot with the profusion of
bright blossoms on the oleanders and poinciana,
and the scent of hibiscus was heavy on the still air.
In the distance, the blue of sea and sky met at the
horizon, unbroken by the sight of land.

Wendy sighed deeply, remembering, but only
for a second or two. Then she gave herself a little
shake and tried to think of the best way to handle
this meeting. She wasn't totally powerless, after all.
She had a will of her own, and Burke certainly
wasn't going to attack her.

She would be pleasant, she decided, but
businesslike and aloof. If he made provocative
remarks she would ignore them, pretend she didn't
understand. If he touched her, came near her, she
would politely ask him not to. If he persisted, she
would simply leave and explain later to Mr Patera
that she couldn't work for a man who made unwelcome advances to her. If that cost her her job, she
would take it as a sign that she should go back to
Baltimore, anyway.

Satisfied with her plan and fortified by this sudden surge of resolution, she stepped firmly off the
brick walk and on to the path of packed sand that
led down to the row of cottages facing the beach.

There were only eight of them, and number
eight, of course, was the farthest one. Even though
Wendy was wearing her coolest blouse—a thin

white batiste, sleeveless, with a low cut square neckline and eyelet inserts—she was beginning to perspire by the time she reached Burke's cottage.

She was glad she had pinned her thick dark hair up on top of her head that morning instead of letting it lie heavily around her face. That helped, but her sandals were full of gritty sand and she was drooping with the heat as she turned into the brick path that led to the door of the cottage.

It was a low pink stucco house with a red tile roof. Here, too, were palm trees and oleander, hibiscus and bougainvillaea. There were two small patches of emerald green lawn in front of the shrubbery on either side of the path.

She stepped on to the low, wide porch, and after a second's hesitation, gritted her teeth and rapped firmly on the door.

While she waited, she went over again in her mind the plan she had made on her way down for handling him if he proved troublesome.

When she heard footsteps coming towards her on the other side of the door, she lifted her head high and put on her most professional expression.

The door opened, then, and he stood there, tall, imposing-looking, his face grim.

'Oh, Wendy,' he said absently, 'come in.'

She stepped inside. The interior was cool and dim. There was green straw matting on the floor, a few pieces of white rattan furniture, and in one corner, by the glass doors to the patio, a large battered desk covered with papers.

Wendy stood primly just inside the door, waiting, watching him carefully. He was dressed casually in tan cotton twill trousers and a darker tan cotton shirt that buttoned down the front. He looked rumpled, she thought, and needed a haircut.

He ran a hand distractedly through his thick dark hair and pointed accusingly at the littered desk.

'That damned machine,' he muttered. 'I never did trust it. I missed two whole days of work, and now the machine breaks down just when I need it.'

Serves you right, Wendy thought unkindly, for fooling around with your blonde friend instead of working. Aloud, she said sweetly, 'That's a shame. I'm quite familiar with these machines. Would you like me to take a look at it?'

'I'd be eternally grateful,' he breathed. 'It's right over here.'

She followed him over to the desk, where the offending tape recorder sat. Wendy set down the package she was carrying and leaned over to inspect the machine.

'Well, it's plugged in, anyway,' she said. She switched it on. Nothing happened. 'A light should go on,' she muttered.

'Oh, that's been broken for a long time,' he announced.

She pressed the rewind button. Nothing happened. Then the fast forward button. Still no activity. She glanced up at him with a sigh.

'I'm afraid it's dead,' she said.

'That's my conclusion, too,' he said dismally. 'Hell. Just when I'd got used to the damned thing.' He gave her an accusing look, as though somehow it was her fault.

'Well, I'm sorry your machine is broken,' she said defensively. 'You'll just have to get along without it. Mr Patera says there's no hope of even getting it to Miami for repairs until Monday.'

'I know,' he said plaintively. 'And then lord only knows how long it will take.' He rubbed a hand over his chin and jawline. 'No point crying over spilt milk,' he said abruptly. 'We might as well get to work. You can sit at the desk.' He pushed aside some of the litter of papers to make room for her. 'I'll pace.'

CHAPTER SEVEN

THEY worked steadily through what remained of the afternoon. Burke was as competent a dictator in person as he was on the machine. His voice was low-pitched, he enunciated clearly, and he dictated at a steady pace, just slow enough so that Wendy had no trouble keeping up with him.

Occasionally, he would hesitate, refer to some notes, or just stand at the glass doors staring out at some unseen object, deep in thought, a frown on his striking features. Then, suddenly, the phrase or passage would come to him. His features would relax, and he would turn around and take up where he left off, sometimes asking her to read back the previous sentence or paragraph.

These short hiatuses gave Wendy a chance to rest her hand, which was developing a writer's cramp. Finally, during one thoughtful spell that lasted longer than usual, Burke turned suddenly to look at her and saw her painfully flexing her fingers.

He glanced at his watch. 'Lord,' he exclaimed, 'it's seven o'clock! What time did you get here?'

'Oh, I don't know,' she replied. 'Some time between three and four.'

'I'm sorry, Wendy,' he apologised. 'I don't usually get so carried away. Poor kid, I'll bet you're starved.' He smiled a little bleakly. 'Probably had a date with your handsome young man, too.'

Wendy murmured non-committally that it was all right, no problem.

'Well,' Burke said briskly, 'I do apologise. I got carried away. I do much better and work faster dictating in person than using that damned machine, anyway.' He looked at her anxiously. 'You did get it all, didn't you?'

She smiled. 'Oh, yes. Don't worry about that.'

He ran a hand through his hair again and began to pace around the room. 'Tell you what,' he said. 'Can you get that typed up in a morning?' She nodded. 'Good,' he went on. 'Type it up tomorrow morning, send it down with the waiter when he brings my lunch at noon. I'll go through it in the early afternoon, then if you can come back around three we can move ahead.'

Wendy hesitated, looking down at her pad. Tomorrow was Saturday. Did he realise that?

'Oh, hell,' he said suddenly, 'it's the weekend, isn't it?' He frowned. 'Well, I guess it'll have to wait until Monday.'

Wendy wondered whether he said that in deference to her or because he had plans of his own. She had nothing special to do over the weekend. She wasn't so sure she wanted Burke Flint to know that, but by now she was so deeply interested in his book that she wanted to continue working.

She stood up and flipped her notebook shut. 'I have no plans for the weekend,' she said in a businesslike tone. 'If you like, I can keep on with it.'

His face lit up. 'That's great. I really appreciate that, Wendy.'

She gathered up her pencils and started towards

the door. He followed her and opened it for her. The sun was going down, lighting up the western sky. Wendy blinked at the sudden brightness after the comparative dimness of the cottage.

She stepped outside, then turned to say goodbye. He was leaning casually against the doorframe, gazing at her, an odd smile on his face.

'I must say I'm surprised you have no plans for the weekend,' he remarked. 'I was sure your young man would be monopolising all your time by now.'

Wendy felt a surge of irritation. 'I don't know why you insist on calling him *my* young man. I only went out with him once.'

Burke grinned and raised one eyebrow. 'Is that right?' he drawled. 'Interesting.'

Wendy could have bitten her tongue out for telling him that. He had been fishing, she realised, for just that information.

'Goodnight, Burke,' she said tersely. 'I'll see you tomorrow afternoon.'

She stalked off down the walk and around the cottages. Not for worlds would she have looked back. Why, she thought angrily, did he continually try to provoke her? Fishing for information like that about her private life so shamelessly!

It wasn't until she was back at the hotel and in her room that it occurred to her to wonder just why he was fishing.

She went into the bathroom to wash her face and comb her hair before going to the employees' dining room for dinner. He wouldn't have done that, she thought, if he hadn't been interested.

She stared at her reflection in the bathroom mirror as she tidied her hair. But what did he want from her? She made a face at herself. Surely you know the answer to that, stupid, she said silently to herself.

Eating dinner alone, she couldn't get the puzzle out of her head. Even later, after she had showered and settled in bed with her book, she couldn't figure it out.

She put the book aside, switched off the lamp, and lay back on the pillow. Number one, she reasoned, he's made it obvious that he's got one thing on his mind as far as I'm concerned, and he seems to be still interested. Otherwise, why would he have forced her to admit that John Frazier was nothing special to her?

Yet, on the other hand, he had been a perfect gentleman that afternoon, had been all business, hadn't made one suggestive move or remark. And, she thought wryly, just when I had myself all primed to resist him and put him in his place.

Was it all part of his cat and mouse game, she wondered. And what about the blonde? Where did she fit in?

Wendy sighed and rolled over on to her stomach. It was getting too confusing for her. She would just do her work and give up these idle speculations.

She formed an image in her mind of John Frazier, with his frank blue eyes, boyish grin and handsome features. There was a man you could feel safe with, she thought.

But as she drifted off into sleep, her conscious will lulled into quiescence, that picture dissolved imperceptibly into a darker face, a sombre expression, a dangerous glint of cold grey eyes and a thin sardonic mouth.

*

Over the next two days, Saturday and Sunday, they fell naturally into a smooth working relationship. Right after breakfast, in the morning, Wendy typed up the previous day's dictation. Then afterwards, she would read over the draft manuscript, check her list of names for spellings, and make any necessary corrections.

After a late lunch, she would take a walk or go for a swim. Then at three o'clock she would walk down to Burke's cottage, where they would work steadily until seven or so.

Burke seemed totally absorbed in his work. He treated Wendy as a necessary adjunct to that work, unfailingly polite, but still so intent on the book that nothing at all of a personal nature passed between them. He never mentioned her 'young man' again.

Wendy found the experience tiring but exhilarating. She became totally absorbed in the book, in the sheer creative mental power in the tall, abstracted man, who paced to and fro in the small living room dictating to her.

On Sunday afternoon, before Wendy left the hotel with her day's pile of manuscript to go to the cottage, John Frazier called and asked her to have dinner with him that night.

'Oh, John,' she said, 'I'd love to, but I've been slaving all weekend on a special project for one of the guests. In fact, I was just on my way there when you called.'

'Surely you have to eat,' he objected.

'Yes, but I've been working until seven o'clock every night. By then I'm so tired I usually just have a light supper in the employees' dining room, read for a while, then fall in bed.'

There was a short silence on the other end of the line. Then, 'What is this project that's keeping you so busy?' he asked.

Wendy hesitated. Should she tell him? Then she thought, Why not? I have nothing to hide.

'One of the guests,' she said finally, 'is writing a book. His tape recorder broke and he needs someone to take dictation.'

Another silence. 'Is that "someone" Burke Flint, by any chance?' he asked.

'How did you know?' Wendy exclaimed before she could stop and think.

'Oh, hotel gossip gets around,' he replied vaguely. 'That was the guy who cut in on us last weekend, wasn't it?'

'My,' she said, laughing, 'you are well-informed.' She glanced at her watch. 'Listen, John, I've got to run. He's expecting me any minute now, and you know these temperamental artists.'

'Okay,' he said, 'but I still say you've got to eat. Why don't I come over around seven and we can eat there? We don't have to make a night of it. What do you say?'

'Well,' Wendy hedged. 'All right.' It would be nice, she thought, to have some pleasant company, to talk to someone about something besides the book.

'Good,' John said quickly. 'I'll meet you at the coffee shop around seven.'

They said goodbye then, and Wendy grabbed the pile of manuscript and hurried down to the cottage.

*

It seemed to her that Burke was having difficulties with his dictating this afternoon. There were long pauses between sentences, as though he were searching for the right phrase and couldn't find it. His frown was thunderous, his pacing almost frantic. When the words did come, they were abrupt, clipped, almost strangulated.

Finally, at about six o'clock, after he had been standing at the patio doors for several minutes staring out, his hands in his trouser pockets, his shoulders hunched over, he turned around and sighed deeply.

'Sorry, Wendy,' he said, looking bleak. 'It's just no good. The words won't come.' He put a hand on the back of his neck and rubbed distractedly.

'You probably just need a rest from it for a while,' she said. 'You've been at it pretty steadily for three days now. Maybe your mind is telling you it's tired and is pleading for a little rest.'

Wearily he sank into one of the rattan armchairs, his legs extended straight out before him. He put his hands behind his head and leaned back, closing his eyes.

Wendy waited, wondering if he had gone to sleep. Should she leave or stay? She got up from the desk and walked over to him. She stood over him, looking down at him, her heart turning over and over.

In repose he looked so vulnerable, she thought, and much, much more handsome without that sardonic look on his face. Her features softened with tenderness as she watched him. She longed to reach out and touch the flat planes of his cheekbones, to smooth back the lock of dark hair that had fallen over his forehead, giving him an unfamiliar boyish look.

Suddenly, his eyes flew open and he was staring straight into hers. Their gaze held for several seconds, seconds that Wendy, held immobile in that penetrating gaze, measured by the pounding of her heart.

She didn't dare look away, but she found that gaze more and more painful every second. Her knees felt weak, and she was having difficulty breathing.

Finally, he gave himself a little shake and sat up abruptly.

'What time is it, anyway?' he said. His voice seemed distant, muted by the pounding in her ears.

He glanced at his watch. Without willing it, Wendy's eyes followed his, and she found herself staring at the watch on his wrist, at his large hand held so gracefully, and the silky black hairs on his forearm curled around the black leather band.

'Good lord,' he said. 'It's after six—time to call it a day.'

The spell was broken, and Wendy crossed over to the desk to gather her things. She sensed his eyes following her and the flesh on her back felt prickly and warm.

Then his voice came to her. 'Would you like to stay and have some supper with me?' he said at last. 'I usually have something sent down, but there are eggs in the fridge and a lot of canned stuff in the cupboard.'

Wendy stood leaning over the desk as though paralysed. Everything in her wanted to stay. She knew she was playing with fire, but so powerful was the attraction of this man that when she was with him her will seemed to drain out of her like water through a sieve.

Then she remembered her date with John Frazier. With a silent mingled sigh of relief and regret, she turned to face him.

'I can't,' she said. 'I have a date.'

He thought for a moment, his face expressionless. 'I see,' he said, and stood up. 'The young man?' She nodded, and he smiled. 'Maybe another time, then,' he said vaguely.

'Yes,' she said dully. All she wanted now was to get out of there.

He followed her to the door and opened it for her. She stepped out into the bright sunshine.

'I'm not sure whether my Muse has deserted me permanently or not,' he said. 'Why don't you type up what you have and, unless you hear from me, come back at three tomorrow.'

'All right,' she said. She turned quickly and went off down the walk, still in a daze. Before she reached the beach path, she heard the front door shut quietly behind her.

'So,' John Frazier said, 'how is the great man's book coming? Making progress?'

It was after dinner, and they were sitting in the employees' dining room over coffee.

'It was coming along quite well before today,' she replied with a smile, 'but it suddenly went sour. I think he's just tired, or has a writer's block, or something.'

John tilted his chair back and braced himself with his feet. 'Or maybe you distract him.'

She coloured and laughed to hide her confusion. 'Oh, I dobt that,' she said. 'I don't think Burke Flint would ever get ruffled by a girl like me.'

He gazed at her over his coffee cup. 'I don't know why you say that. You're a very beautiful, very desirable girl. And that night over at the Seacliff, he seemed very determined to get you off alone.'

She shrugged and said carefully, 'I think he's the kind of man who likes to play games with any reasonably presentable woman. It's his nature.'

John frowned, and leaned forward, his elbows on the table. 'Maybe. Somehow I don't like the idea of you down there alone with him in that cottage every day.'

She had to laugh at that. 'Believe me, John, he's all business when he's working. His book means more to him than any woman, I think. I'm no more than a machine to him.'

His face cleared then, and he seemed relieved. 'Do you want to go for a swim, or a walk?' he asked, rising from his chair.

She glanced at her watch. It was almost ten. 'I don't think so. It's late. I had no idea we'd been here for three hours.'

The evening had passed swiftly. They seemed to have a lot to say to each other, recounting their past histories, telling each other about their families and friends. Wendy hadn't mentioned David when he'd asked her if she had ever been really in love. She only said that she'd thought so once, but it hadn't worked out. He didn't question her further.

'Well, I'll walk you to your room, anyway,' he said.

The corridor was deserted and dim. As they

passed Meg's door, Wendy wondered if she and Ken had come back from Miami. If so, they were probably out together somewhere. Wendy envied them.

Wendy unlocked the door to her room and turned to say goodnight to John. As she did so, she found that he had spread his arms wide, bracing them on either side of the doorsill.

She looked up at him. The blue, blue eyes shone down on her, a look of tenderness in the handsome face.

'Wendy,' he said in a husky voice, and bent down to kiss her lightly on the mouth. 'I could get to be very fond of you if you'd let me,' he murmured, putting his hands on her shoulders.

'John,' she began, 'I . . . you'll have to give me some time. I'm a little confused right now.'

'Sure,' he said swiftly. He gave her shoulders a quick squeeze and stood back from her. 'I understand. You haven't forgotten the party next weekend?'

'No, of course not,' she replied. 'I'm looking forward to it. Goodnight, then, John, and thanks for a pleasant evening.'

She slipped inside then, and closed and locked the door. She leaned back against it for several minutes, thinking of John Frazier, his kindness and consideration, his good looks, his obvious interest in her. Was he the good, dull man who would take care of her, be good to her, make her happy?

Could be, she thought, as she got ready for bed. But what about the quickening pulse and rush of passion? Would that come in time?

As she slipped into bed and reached over to turn

out the light, her eyes fell on Burke's book, face down on the nightstand so that his photograph on the back cover stared up at her. Her heart gave a great lurch, and it seemed to her those piercing grey eyes could penetrate into the deepest recesses of her heart, into her very soul.

The next morning Meg was in the office before Wendy, and as soon as she saw her she began to recount the events of her weekend with Ken's parents, burbling on and on, happy and content.

'And, Wendy, I had the feeling they liked me, I mean *really* liked me,' she finished up with an ecstatic look on her face.

'Well, of course they liked you,' Wendy commented, amused. 'Why shouldn't they?'

She opened her shorthand notebook and rolled in a fresh sheet of draft paper in her typewriter to transcribe yesterday's notes.

'Hey, what's going on?' Meg asked. 'How come the shorthand?'

Wendy explained about the broken tape recorder and how she had spent the weekend working on Burke Flint's book. Meg listened, fascinated.

'Did he make a pass at you?' she asked.

'Of course not, Meg,' Wendy said, a little annoyed. 'He's all business when he's working.'

'That's too bad,' Meg said drily. She began to examine the work on her desk. 'Did you see John over the weekend?' she asked casually as she flipped through the top folder.

'Yes, we had dinner together last night,' Wendy replied.

Meg darted an interested glance at her. 'Do you like him?'

'Very much. He's easy to be with. Good company.'

'Doesn't sound very exciting,' Meg commented.

'I've had enough of excitement,' Wendy said firmly. 'It's too unnerving.' She turned to her notebook. 'Listen, Meg, I've got to get started on my notes before they're stone cold.'

That afternoon, Wendy started off for Burke's cottage a little before three. Since noon, dark thunderclouds had begun to appear and by now the sky was filled with an ominous and forbidding mass.

It was oppressively warm and still as Wendy stepped outside, and the rain had begun to spatter down in fat heavy drops. The whole landscape was changed. The sea looked dull and oily, the beach drab and deserted, the greenery dull and somehow shrunken.

Wendy had put a scarf over her head and wrapped her work in a plastic sack. As she walked down the brick path to the beach, the heavens opened up and the rain came pouring down. In seconds she was soaked to the skin.

She started to run. The brick path was slippery from the rain, so she moved carefully, awkwardly, carefully placing her sandals. Once she was on the sandy beach path, her footing felt more secure, and she flew down to the row of cottages, around in front of them, then started up the brick walk to Burke's cottage.

By now her blue skirt was sodden, and flapped heavily around her legs, impeding her progress. Her thin white blouse clung to her like a second skin, and even the lacy bra underneath was soaked.

As she raced up the brick walk leading to the

door of the cottage, there was a sudden crack of lightning followed immediately by a roar of thunder. Wendy, in a panic, her drenched skirt like a dead weight around her knees, put on a sudden sprint, stumbled, and fell, in the next second lying sprawled face down on the bricks, the rain pouring down on her, a searing pain in her right knee.

Luckily, the plastic-wrapped package had fallen first and landed just where her head hit the ground, cushioning the blow and protecting her face from bruising.

The door of the cottage flew open and Burke came running out. He scooped Wendy up in his arms, grabbing the plastic package as he did so, and carried her into the house, kicking the door shut behind him.

He stood, still holding her, in the middle of the living room, looking down at her with concern. Wendy clung to him, her arms wound tightly around his neck, her head buried in his shoulder.

Gradually, the panic began to subside. She loosened her hold on him and gave him a sheepish look.

'You can put me down, now,' she said. 'I think I skinned my knee, but otherwise I'm all right.'

Burke gave her a relieved smile. 'I'm glad to hear that, but I rather like this arrangement myself.'

Wendy coloured as his gaze left her face to travel down the length of her body. With her soaked clothing clinging to her, very little was left to the imagination.

With a little laugh he set her down on her feet. Immediately, a puddle began to form on the straw matting and blood flowed down her leg from the cut on her knee.

'Oh, dear,' she said, 'I'm ruining your floor.'

'Here,' he said briskly, 'you've got to get those clothes off.'

She gave him a startled look, and he made an impatient gesture.

'In the bathroom,' he said sarcastically. 'Come on.'

Meekly she followed him through a small, neat bedroom into a white-tiled, good-sized bathroom. He flipped the switch on the wall radiator, and pointed to a rack of clean white towels. He went into the bedroom for a moment and came back with a dark blue dressing gown, which he hung up on the back of the door.

'There,' he said, 'you're all set. Clothes off, get in the shower, then on with the dressing gown while your clothes dry. Bandages in the medicine cabinet for your knee. Okay? Need any help?'

She smiled. 'Yes, okay. No, I don't need any help.'

He gave her a mock salute and left, leaving Wendy to shut and lock the bathroom door behind him.

She stripped off her sodden clothes and got under the hot shower. After she had dried herself she slipped on the dark blue dressing gown, belting it securely in front. She had to laugh when she looked in the mirror at the way Burke's dressing gown hung on her. She rolled up the cuffs of the sleeves and cinched the belt tighter.

She draped her skirt, blouse and underwear on the shower curtain rod, then sat down on the edge of the tub, wondering nervously whether to venture out of the bathroom or sit there until her clothes dried.

On second thoughts, that seemed like a silly thing to do—it could take hours. There came a sharp rapping on the door just then, and startled, Wendy jumped and almost fell off the edge of the bathtub.

'Are you decent?' came Burke's voice. 'Come on out and have a cup of tea. I'll be in the kitchen. There's a small clothes dryer there.'

She heard his retreating footsteps, and gathering up her wet clothes in the bath towel she had used, she opened the door and stepped into Burke Flint's very plain, almost sombrely monk-like bedroom.

She could hear him at a distance as he puttered around in the kitchen, the clink of dishes, the whistling of a tea kettle, and his own husky baritone humming off-key.

She couldn't resist a look around the clean, orderly bedroom. There was a double bed—of course, she thought to herself—a wooden chest of drawers with a small mirror on the top and a set of silver-backed brushes.

There was a nightstand with a good reading light by the side of the bed. Sitting on top of it was a framed photograph. Her curiosity aroused, Wendy crossed over to it to get a better look.

It was a photograph of two men and a girl dressed in some kind of rumpled drab battle fatigues and taken in a tropical setting. One of the men was a younger Burke Flint, the other was not familiar, and the girl was the blonde who had been with

Burke at the Seacliff that night. She was standing between the two men, her arms around their waists, laughing at the camera.

Wendy drew in her breath sharply. The picture opened up vistas of Burke's past that he had shared with this woman, years when Wendy hadn't known he'd existed, much less been so fatally attracted to him.

She was so intent on the photograph, she failed to notice that the noises coming from the kitchen had ceased, until a prickly sensation at the back of her neck warned her that someone was staring at her.

'See anything interesting?' Burke drawled.

She whirled around to see him leaning casually against the doorframe, his arms folded across his chest, a smug, amused look on his face.

They stared at each other for several moments. Then Wendy flushed and dropped her eyes from that sardonic, penetrating gaze.

'I—I'm sorry,' she faltered. 'I didn't mean to pry.'

Slowly he came towards her, his eyes never leaving her face. When he was only inches away from her, he reached out and picked up the photograph. He stared intently at it for a moment, then held it up in front of Wendy.

'Well,' he said, 'what do you think?'

'About what?' she stammered, staring at the picture, sedulously avoiding his eyes.

'Why, about this glimpse of my past,' he said. His voice was amused.

Wendy glanced up at him, aware now that he was teasing her. She was relieved that he wasn't annoyed at her prying, but beginning to grow angry at his condescending tone.

'I think she's very lovely, and that you look very happy together,' she said finally, in a cool tone.

'We were,' he agreed seriously. 'Very happy.' Wendy's heart sank. He set the photograph back down on the nightstand and turned to her.

'Are you jealous?' he asked.

'Of course not,' she retorted, her eyes blazing.

'Because if you are, I just thought you might be interested to know that the other man in the picture is my brother, and Andrea is his wife.' His mouth twitched, then broke into a wide grin. 'They are still quite happily married and have three strapping young sons, one of whom is named after me.'

Wendy went livid with rage. She stamped her foot. 'You!' she cried. 'You . . . you . . . !' She couldn't think of a name bad enough to call him.

By now he had thrown his head back and was laughing heartily. Wendy stared at the long, strong column of his throat, the open neck of his shirt, and longed to dig her fingernails into his skin, to draw blood.

She had whirled around and had started to walk away from him, when she felt herself caught in an iron grip. He had grabbed her by the shoulders so suddenly that she lost her balance and fell heavily back against him.

Instantly her anger evaporated as she felt his hands leave her shoulders, slide slowly down her arms and then clasp her about the waist. She sighed deeply and closed her eyes. Her body went limp as she leaned against him. She felt his head come down, his face buried in her hair.

Then his cheek was on hers, his mouth at her ear. 'Wendy,' he said in a low voice.

The room began to spin. She opened her eyes, fighting for control. He was nibbling now at her ear, his warm breath soft and teasing. His hands were gently kneading her midriff, the silky material of the dark dressing gown sliding sensuously over her bare skin.

She gathered together all her power of will, put her hands on his, and tried to pull away from his grasp.

'No,' he murmured in her ear. In one swift movement he had turned her around so that she was facing him. He folded his arms around her and just held her close, unmoving, his chin resting on the top of her head.

She could hear his heart steadily beating under her ear, smell the clean soapy smell of his crisp white cotton shirt, feel the hardness of his chest as she lay against it. She sighed again.

His hand came up under her chin and tilted her head back so that she was looking up into his face.

CHAPTER EIGHT

'Do you remember the first time we met?' he murmured.

She couldn't speak. She looked up into his eyes, drowning in those grey pools. Her throat was constricted. She could only nod.

'I thought you were a mermaid,' he said dreamily. His hand was stroking her back in a gentle rhythmic motion as he spoke.

She watched, wide-eyed, as his face bent down to hers, saw the thin mouth, softened now with desire, the glittering eyes. Then his mouth was on hers, soft and sweet. Her arms crept up around his neck and she ran her hands through the thick dark hair, moulding his skull.

His breath quickened at her touch, and his kiss hardened, became more demanding, probing. She responded totally, arching her back, straining her body against his, her lips parting in an ecstasy of surrender.

As though dancing in perfect harmony, and still clinging together, their mouths joined, they moved slowly towards the bed and sank slowly down upon it. Leaning over her, Burke eased her shoulders down on the bed, then lifted his head.

'I don't want to frighten you, Wendy,' he whispered.

She smiled and shook her head slowly from side to side. 'I'm not frightened,' she whispered back.

What she longed to say, what she felt deeply, was, I love you. But the words wouldn't come.

He laid his hand on her neck then, and slowly, his eyes never leaving hers, slid it down the length of her body, lingering tantalisingly over her breasts. When his hand reached her waist, he began to untie the belt, glancing quickly at her face, as if for permission. She smiled at him.

He finished untying the belt, and, leaving the openings of the robe together so that it still covered her, began to unbutton his shirt. Wendy put a hand on his.

'Let me,' she whispered, amazed at her own brazen audacity.

He leaned over closer. Slowly, with delicious intimacy, she began to undo the front of his crisp white shirt. Then, deliberately, she ran the tips of her fingers down over his chest.

He gave a little gasp of pleasure, then straightened up. Slowly, he pushed aside the edges of the dressing gown so that her full breasts were exposed before him. For a few moments he only sat and feasted his eyes on the sight. Then he reached out both hands and moved them over the white mounds and their stiffening points.

Wendy had never before in her life experienced anything like the exquisite waves of pleasure that coursed through her at his touch, and when he bent his head to taste the soft white flesh, she moaned aloud with delight. Instinctively, without volition, she reached down and put her hands on the dark head, pulling him closer to her breast, and gasped as his mouth drew hungrily at the hard, thrusting nipple.

Then he pulled himself up so that he lay on top of her, his mouth crushing hers. She slid her hands under the shirt and with a now frantic movement, stroked the smooth skin of his back and shoulders, the hard muscles underneath flexing at her touch.

He tore his mouth away from hers and, panting, gazed down at her, stroking the hair back from her forehead.

'I want you, Wendy,' he gasped. 'Oh, God, I want you now.'

'Yes,' she said with a smile. 'Oh, yes, Burke.'

His eyes lit up, then clouded over. 'When you said you were inexperienced,' he said in a tight voice as though fighting for control, 'did you mean totally, or only comparatively?'

'It doesn't matter,' she said.

'I want to know. Now,' he said. 'Before it's too late.'

She turned her head away. 'What difference does it make?' she asked in a small voice.

She felt his body stiffen. 'It may not make any difference to you, but it makes a hell of a lot of difference to me.'

'Why?' she asked, looking up at him again.

'I'll tell you why,' he ground out in a grim tone. 'I have no desire to deflower any virgins, that's why.'

Wendy understood at once. To a man like Burke, such an act would imply some sense of responsibility, of commitment. He obviously didn't want that. She bit her lip and turned her head again. She couldn't lie to him. He'd find out anyway.

'All right,' she said in a muffled voice. She turned

back to him. 'But it doesn't matter,' she pleaded again.

Her heart sank at the harsh look on his face, and she knew the moment was lost. Then his eyes softened, and he smiled regretfully. He pulled the edges of the dressing gown together to cover her, then soberly and deliberately tied the belt securely. He smoothed her tousled hair back from her forehead, gently, tenderly.

'That's too great a gift to give to someone like me, little Wendy,' he said. 'Not now, anyway.' He shook his head, smiling. 'What am I going to do about you?'

Wendy sat up, pulling the dressing gown tighter around her. 'Don't patronise me, Burke,' she said in an even tone. 'I'm not a child.' Now that the passion of a moment ago had been crushed, she was growing angry.

She swung her legs around and got up off the bed. She went to the window and pulled the curtain aside, staring out at the sea, deep in thought. She had wanted Burke's good opinion, his respect, his love. It had only brought her frustration and disappointment. She had lost, she knew that now.

He would never love her as she wanted to be loved, she thought, and he wouldn't take her because he thought of her as an inexperienced young girl, a burden he had no intention of taking on.

I'm twenty-five years old, she thought bitterly. It seems the men I want, I can't have, at least not on a permanent basis. More than anything, now, she wanted to erase from Burke Flint's mind forever that hateful image of her as a retarded child.

She made up her mind, then took a deep breath,

and turned around to face him. His shirt was still unbuttoned, his hair rumpled, and he was staring at her with an inscrutable look.

'I want you to know,' she said evenly, 'that before I came here I was involved with a married man.' Odd, she thought as the words left her mouth, how much satisfaction she now derived from uttering that dreadful secret aloud.

His gaze never wavered, but the grey eyes widened a little. 'I see,' he said. He got up and walked over to the dresser. He lit a cigarette, inhaled deeply, and turned to face her. 'So you lied just now,' he said. 'You're not a virgin.'

She waved a hand in the air and frowned. 'No, I didn't lie.'

'Then why are you telling me this?' he asked.

Wendy drew herself up to her full height, determined now to go on. 'Because I want you to quit treating me like a child,' she almost shouted, glaring at him.

He stared at her for a moment, their eyes locked together, then threw back his head and laughed. He stubbed out his cigarette, then crossed over to her. He put an arm around her shoulders and kissed her lightly on the forehead.

'Wendy, Wendy,' he said. 'You're full of surprises. What am I going to do with you?'

'I told you,' she muttered, 'quit treating me like a child.'

He laughed again and released her. 'Come on,' he said, 'let's get those wet clothes in the dryer and have that cup of tea. Then you can tell me all about your wild past.'

*

They sat in the little kitchen, drinking tea and waiting for Wendy's clothes to dry. Wendy told him briefly and truthfully about her romance with David. She was amazed to find how easily the words came. He listened silently, gravely, and at the end, merely asked, 'Do you still love him?'

Wendy shook her head. 'No. That's over.'

After that, by tacit mutual consent, they stayed off inflammatory subjects.

To Wendy's pleased surprise, Burke began to talk about himself. His father, now dead, had been in the military, a colonel in the Air Force. Burke and his brother, Tom, had come along late in life for his parents. His father had been away on tours of duty much of the time, and his mother had always travelled with him when she could, preparing a home for him, leaving the two young boys in expensive private schools.

'It sounds like a lonely childhood,' Wendy said with sympathy.

He gave her a surprised look. 'Not really,' he said. 'I was good at sports—the open sesame to life in a boys' school.' He grinned. 'I was a good fighter, too, big and strong for my age, and I never had any trouble getting good grades.' His grin widened. 'Of course, I got into my share of mischief, and I'm not sure my teachers were ever sorry to see me move out of their classes. But I never had a problem getting along with the other boys.'

Her eyes twinkling, she asked, 'And what about girls?'

He smiled slyly. 'Oh, that's another story. I'll save that for the next chapter.'

'I can imagine it will be fascinating—and instructive,' she commented drily. 'Yet, you've never married?'

'Nope,' he said abruptly. 'Never had the time. I was always too busy travelling around, getting myself in trouble.'

Wendy toyed with her empty cup. 'You've been in some dangerous situations, haven't you?'

He waved a hand in the air and tilted his chair back. 'Not really,' he said briefly. 'Besides, I thrive on danger.'

The small portable dryer in the corner of the kitchen suddenly switched off just then. Wendy jumped up and crossed over to it, reaching inside to make sure her clothes were dry. She pulled them out.

'I'd better get dressed now and get back to the hotel,' she said on her way to the bedroom. 'Meg will be wondering what happened to me.'

As she dressed, she couldn't help wondering what the future would hold for her and Burke Flint. Would there even be a future? He had told her that afternoon when they were discussing his work that when the book on Poland was finished he was going on an assignment for a magazine to Palestine to do a series of articles on the Middle East. Would he then vanish from her life?

When she went back to the kitchen, Burke was standing at the sink, his arms braced on the draining board, staring out of the window. He seemed to be deep in thought.

'I'd better be going,' she said.

He turned around and gave her an odd look, frowning and smiling at the same time. He walked towards her, put his hands on her shoulders and looked down at her.

'All right,' he said, gently kneading her shoulders. 'I don't think I want to work tomorrow. I'll call you around five-thirty. Maybe we can go for a swim, then out to dinner somewhere later. How does that sound?'

It sounded like heaven, she said to herself. Aloud, she said evenly, 'That sounds fine.'

The next day passed agonisingly slowly. Wendy tried to keep busy. Luckily, the work-load was beginning to pick up and she didn't have much time during the day to think about the date with Burke that evening.

Occasionally, in spite of her best efforts, she would be sitting at her desk and suddenly wake up to the fact that she had been staring out of the window for some time. Meg was so wrapped up in her own affairs that she didn't even notice.

Finally, five o'clock did arrive. In an agony of nervous apprehension, she straightened her desk and put the cover on her typewriter. She said a brief goodnight to Meg and went off to her own room.

The minute she stepped inside, the telephone began to ring. She stared at it for a few moments, then swiftly crossed the room to answer it.

It was Burke. 'Are you ready?' he asked lightly.

Her mind went blank at the sound of his voice. 'Ready for what?' she asked.

'Don't tell me you've forgotten already,' he said with a sigh. 'What a fickle woman! One day and she's forgotten my existence.'

'Believe me, Burke, I haven't forgotten your existence,' she said.

'Then get down here now,' he commanded, a note of gravity now in his bantering tone. 'Tell you what. Get on your swimsuit and meet me at that little cove. It's sheltered from the sun and very few people go there.'

With fumbling fingers, Wendy got undressed and into her string-coloured bikini. She slipped on her white terrycloth robe and sandals and hurried off down to the beach.

He was waiting for her at the end of the path, where it curved around the stand of palm trees to the little cove. When she first caught sight of him, she drew in her breath sharply at his tall lean muscular frame in the dark swimming trunks, a white towel slung casually around his neck.

He was leaning up against a tree trunk smoking a cigarette. When he saw her he bent over and snuffed out his cigarette in the sand. Then he started walking slowly towards her, and she felt suddenly shy. She stood still, waiting for him. Then he was standing before her, and all she could think of was how she longed to throw her arms around him, to feel him close to her.

He leaned over and kissed her gently, lightly on the mouth. 'Did you miss me?' he asked with a grin.

Her shyness vanished. 'Of course not,' she said airily. She walked past him towards the beach. As she passed by, out of the corner of her eye she could see the incredulous look on his face.

'Why, you little . . .' he muttered, and reached out a hand to stop her.

She slipped out of his grasp and, laughing, began to run. The little beach was deserted. Quickly, she took off her robe and sandals and looked back. He was walking slowly towards her, arms akimbo.

She laughed again, then, with a little thrill of fear at the grim set of his mouth and flashing eyes, she ran towards the sea and began to swim away.

It wasn't long before he caught up with her, and she felt his strong arms grasp her from behind in a vice-like grip.

With a sudden, powerful movement, he whirled her around in the water and lifted her high up in front of him, his hands at her waist. His eyes gleamed with desire and his lip curled with mock severity as he crushed her slippery body against his. She arched her back, wriggling to get free of his imprisoning grip, her head thrown back in laughter.

The sudden movement and the weight of the water pulled the scanty bra of her bikini down so that it barely covered her. When she twisted around in his arms she felt his hands slide up her midriff to rest possessively on her almost bare breasts.

She quit struggling then, and leaned back against him with a sigh of pleasure. Then, suddenly, he released her and began swimming away from her.

'Come on, mermaid,' he called. 'Play with me.'

Later, they got dressed—Wendy in her room and Burke in his cottage—and went to a restaurant in downtown Nassau for dinner. Wendy was amazed at how comfortable she felt with him now. He was attentive and courteous, with only an occasional hint of the old superior, mocking arrogance, in a certain way he had of looking at her, or the tone of his voice.

He told her over dinner about some problems he

was having with his editor in New York over the
publication date of his book and his participation in
the promotion of it.

'They want to publish it as soon as it's finished,'
he explained, 'and put me on talk shows like some
damned entertaining animal.'

'And what do you want?' she asked. Privately
she thought that any talk show host would have a
difficult time getting any entertainment value out of
this man if he had made up his mind not to co-
operate.

'I want what I've always wanted,' he said firmly.
'To finish the job in hand and get on to the next
assignment.'

She smiled. 'Then I'm sure that's exactly what
you'll do.'

He raised his eyebrows at her. 'You're beginning
to know me too well,' he remarked. 'I'm not sure I
like that.'

Throughout the rest of the evening, he was
obviously putting himself out to be amusing and
polite, but he barely touched her, and not a word of
intimacy passed between them.

They left the restaurant early and drove back to
the hotel in silence. Wendy had begun to wonder if
she had dreamed that only the day before she had
lain in his arms. Burke seemed a thousand miles
away, lost in his own thoughts.

At the door to her room, she fumbled with her
key, wondering if he was going to let her go without
a touch, without a word. She turned to him to
say goodnight, and by the dim light of the corridor she could see him looking down at her, frowning.

'I can't make up my mind what to do about you, little Wendy,' he said softly.

She gazed up at him. 'You don't have to do anything,' she said.

'Oh, yes, I do,' he said under his breath. He put a hand on her cheek. 'I've decided to go to New York tomorrow,' he announced abruptly. 'I've put it off long enough, and now seems like a good time for a variety of reasons. I won't be gone long, and when I come back, we can take up where we left off.'

'With the book, you mean?' she asked demurely.

'Why, you little . . .' he muttered. 'No,' he said, 'not with the book.' He bent down and kissed her lightly on the mouth. 'I'm not one for commitment, Wendy,' he said in a low voice. 'I never have been and probably never will be. I don't want to lose you, but I don't want to hurt you, either.'

She gave him a defiant look. 'I can look after myself,' she said. 'Let me make that decision.'

'Think it over carefully while I'm gone,' he said. 'Then we'll talk about it when I get back.'

She nodded and watched as he walked off down the corridor away from her.

During the time Burke was gone, Wendy tried to keep as busy as possible. At the weekend she went to the party with John Frazier. Meg and Ken went with them, and Wendy was relieved to see that they were too wrapped up in each other to notice how bored and distracted she was.

All she could think about was Burke Flint. She knew she was hopelessly in love with him by now, and she didn't care anything about commitment any more. She wanted him for as long as he wanted her, for as long as she could have him, and she planned to tell him that as soon as he came back.

On Sunday night he called her from New York. She was in her room, getting ready for bed, when the telephone rang. When she heard his voice she almost fainted.

'Burke,' she said breathlessly. 'I didn't expect you to call.'

'I didn't, either,' he said in a grim tone. Then, more gently, 'Damn it, Wendy, I miss you.'

Wendy's heart turned over. She sat down slowly on the edge of the bed, her legs so unsteady she was afraid she would fall.

'I've missed you, too, Burke,' she said in a low voice.

'We're still arguing up here about the publication date,' he went on, 'but I've told them I'm leaving Tuesday. They can just try to settle it without me.'

'Then you'll be back on Tuesday?' That was only two more days. She tried to remain calm, but her voice was trembling with excitement.

'Right. I'll call you as soon as I get back, then.' He said goodbye and hung up.

Wendy carefully replaced the receiver and sat there for several moments in a daze, staring at the telephone. She hardly dared to hope, but she thought she had detected real caring for her in the tone of his voice.

She spent a restless, sleepless night. No matter how she tried, she couldn't keep the images and memories from her restless mind. Burke's tall body, his rare smile, his laugh, the grey eyes that seemed to pierce to her very soul, the feel of his hands on her, his kiss.

She tossed restlessly on her bed, tormented by conflicting feelings about their coming meeting. He said he had missed her, so at least he hadn't forgotten all about her. She longed for the moment when she would see him again, but dreaded it at the same time.

The next day in the office, Meg finally came down to earth long enough to notice that something had happened.

Wendy had asked her first thing in the morning what she could do to help her with the work piled on her desk. Meg gave her a searching look.

'Say,' she said, 'I thought you were working exclusively on Burke Flint's book.'

Wendy laughed. 'Oh, Meg, you really have been out of it. He's been gone since last Wednesday.'

Meg frowned. 'Funny, I hadn't noticed.'

'I'm not surprised,' Wendy said wryly. She crossed over to Meg's desk and began to glance through the folders stacked there. 'Which of these would you like me to take?'

'Oh, it doesn't matter,' Meg said. She was still frowning at Wendy. 'You don't seem broken-hearted that he's gone,' she commented.

Wendy coloured, her eyes fixed firmly on the pile of folders. 'Why should I be?' she asked, trying to sound casual.

Meg's eyes narrowed. 'I'm not sure,' she said at last. 'Only I think there's something you're not telling me.'

Wendy's face grew redder. She laughed, chose some folders at random and walked back to her desk, her flaming cheeks averted from Meg's penetrating gaze.

Meg opened her mouth to speak when the door to the corridor opened and a tall blond man walked inside. He glanced briefly at Meg, then at Wendy, whose back was turned to him.

Meg opened her mouth to speak. 'Can I help . . .' she started to say. But the man took two purposeful strides towards Wendy.

'Wendy?' he said.

She whirled around in her chair and gazed at him in horrified dawning recognition.

'David!' she cried, and put a hand over her mouth.

Meg just stood and stared, wide-eyed, at this sudden apparition. The man ignored her presence. He held out a tentative hand to Wendy, and she shrank back.

'What—what in the world are you doing here?' she whispered.

'I had to come,' he said flatly. Then his glance flicked to Meg and back to Wendy. 'Is there somewhere we can talk?' he said in a low voice.

'No,' Wendy cried. 'No. I'm working. Can't you see? I'm working.' She was on the verge of hysteria, her words disjointed and stumbling.

Meg coughed loudly. 'Uh, I have to see about something,' she muttered as she edged past them towards the door.

She gave Wendy a worried look, as if asking whether or not she wanted her to stay. Wendy had recovered her composure sufficiently to realise that she would just have to deal with the situation. The shock of seeing David here, in Nassau, in the hotel, in the office, had temporarily disoriented her. He didn't *belong* here, she kept thinking. Somehow it was all wrong for him to be here. He belonged to the past, a past she wanted forgotten, dead and buried.

But deal with it she must. She sighed and gave Meg a little nod, and Meg left the room without a backward glance.

Wendy stood up and faced David. 'What do you want?' she asked in a stern tone.

His shoulders slumped forward, and he seemed to look smaller than she remembered him, somehow diminished. He was still the same handsome appealing David, but, gazing at him now, she wondered how she could ever have thought she was in love with him, ever gone through such misery over him.

When he didn't speak, she repeated her question. 'What do you want, David?'

'You know what I want,' he said in a low, intimate tone.

'If you mean what I think you mean, David, you know that's impossible.'

'No,' he said, recovering himself a little, his voice firmer. 'No, it isn't. I've filed for divorce.'

She opened her mouth in horror. 'On what grounds?' she asked, stupefied.

He shrugged. 'You don't need grounds any more. Sheila knows I don't love her any more, haven't loved her for a long time. She's agreed to it.'

'I see,' Wendy said carefully. On no account, she thought, must I give him any encouragement. 'What has that to do with me that you came all this way to tell me about it?'

He stared at her in disbelief. 'It has everything to

do with you,' he cried. 'Why do you think I'm doing it?'

'David, stop that right now,' she said. 'I told you weeks ago I would have no part of that. If you and your wife feel you can't stay married to each other, that's your affair, but leave me out of it.'

He seemed to be having trouble assimilating what she was saying. 'Are you telling me,' he asked slowly, 'that you don't love me any more? That you never loved me?'

She winced at that and crossed over to the window. She stood staring out at the sandy beach, the blue sky, the sea, thinking how to choose the words for an answer.

Had she loved David? Certainly she didn't love him now. She had thought she loved him in the past, but compared to what she felt for Burke Flint, it was nothing, a childish interlude, only a pale prelude to the real thing.

She turned to face him, and her heart softened a little at the stricken look on his face. Even though he had deceived her, she never once doubted that he truly loved her. It just wasn't in her to be brutal.

'Of course I loved you, David,' she said softly, and instantly regretted the words when she saw the way his face lit up.

He took a step towards her, and instinctively, she drew back. He stopped, gave her one agonised, frustrated look and dropped his eyes.

'I know I behaved badly,' he said in a low humble tone. 'I know I didn't play fair with you.' He looked at her remorsefully. 'I deceived you. I don't blame you for not being able to forgive me. But I'll make it up to you if you'll just give me a chance.'

She sighed. 'David, it isn't a question of forgiveness. I do forgive you. It's—just—over.'

'I won't accept that,' he said gruffly. He reached out and took her roughly by the arms, his fingers digging into the bare flesh.

There was a knock on the door. David dropped his hands from Wendy's arms and turned away. Coughing discretely, Meg made her way into the room.

'Ah, sorry,' she stammered, 'but I've got to get at a rush job.' She shot Wendy an apologetic look.

'Of course, Meg,' Wendy said briskly.

She started back to her desk. As she passed by David, he reached out and touched her arm.

'We've got to talk,' he said in a low voice.

'There's nothing more to say,' she muttered without looking at him. 'Please, just go away and leave me alone.'

'I'm staying here at the hotel,' he persisted, as though he hadn't even heard her. 'I'll come back here later this afternoon when you're through work.'

Without replying, she sat down at her desk and began to examine the top folder. David tore his eyes from her, gave Meg a quick glance, and strode out of the room.

Meg practically tiptoed over to her desk when he was gone, as though walking on eggs, hardly daring to make a sound, so explosive did the situation she had blundered into seem.

She looked at Wendy, whose eyes were determinedly fixed on the sheet of paper she was rolling into her typewriter. There was a long silence until, finally, Meg cleared her throat.

'Uh, that was David, I gather,' she said in small voice.

'Yes,' Wendy replied without looking at her, her voice hard. 'It was.'

Another silence, while Meg waited for her to elaborate. Then, timidly Meg said, 'He's very good-looking.'

'Yes,' Wendy said in the same strained tone. 'He is.'

She was extremely shaken by the encounter with David. Seeing him again, comparing him with Burke, she knew without a doubt where her heart lay. She had loved David, but her sense of belong-ingness to Burke was so powerful that any other emotion seemed trivial beside it.

Still, her inner turmoil was no reason to be rude to Meg. She turned to her now and forced out a weak smile.

'Sorry to be so rude, Meg, but it was a terrible shock to me to see him here like that.'

'What are you going to do?' Meg asked.

'Do? I'm not going to do anything. I just want him to leave me alone.'

'He seemed very determined,' Meg said firmly. 'I don't think you're going to get rid of him that easily.'

Wendy gave her a startled look. Meg was right. He had said he'd come back later. For one panicky moment she considered running away, but im-mediately saw how foolish that idea was.

Burke would be back tomorrow night. Somehow she would have to convince David before then to leave Nassau, that she really meant what she said, even if she had to be cruel. It would be disastrous for the two men to meet. She had told Burke about the relationship, but she knew he had only half believed her, that he had thought she was only trying to impress him with her 'experience'.

'I'll get rid of him,' she said between her teeth, 'one way or another.'

Meg gave her a dubious look. 'Well, good luck. I hope you're right.'

CHAPTER NINE

THE two girls worked steadily throughout the rest of the day, and Wendy managed to put David out of her mind entirely. She and Meg had lunch in the coffee shop, and there was no sign of him there.

'Maybe he did leave,' Meg remarked encouragingly over lunch. She had noticed Wendy scanning the room anxiously.

Wendy turned hopeful eyes on her friend. 'Oh, Meg, do you really think so?'

Meg hesitated, her sandwich halfway to her mouth. 'Well, no,' she replied at last, 'not really, to tell you the truth, but what do I know? Let's hope for the best.' She took a bite of her sandwich and gave Wendy a searching look. 'Why are you so anxious to get rid of him, anyway?' she asked.

'Number one, he's still married,' Wendy replied, 'and number two, I honestly can't imagine now what I ever saw in him in the first place.'

'Outside of the fact that he's a very attractive man and obviously crazy about you,' Meg remarked drily.

Wendy dismissed this with a wave of her hand. 'The world is full of attractive men,' she said, 'and David only wants me because he can't have me. He'll survive.'

'What about number three?' Meg asked. Wendy stared at her blankly, uncomprehending. 'Your reasons,' Meg explained, 'for wanting to get rid of him. You only gave two.'

Wendy lowered her eyes and poked at her salad. 'I think that about covers it.'

'I see,' Meg said. 'Burke Flint has nothing to do with any of this.'

Wendy coloured violently. Then she sighed. 'I don't know why I try to hide things from you,' she said with a weak smile. 'I think you're clairvoyant.'

'No,' Meg said, 'only you're more transparent than you realise. Does Burke Flint have anything to do with it?'

'He has everything to do with it,' Wendy admitted. 'He'll be back tomorrow night, and I definitely do not want David and Burke to meet.'

Meg eyed her carefully. 'You've really got it bad, huh?'

Wendy nodded and smiled bleakly. 'I know there's no future in it. Burke made it very clear that he's not the kind of man to make commitments, but I just don't care. I want him on any terms.'

'Be careful, Wendy,' Meg advised soberly. 'A man like Burke Flint could make your experience with David seem like child's play. I admit he's tempting, but please be careful. You're not the kind of girl to be satisfied with a casual affair.'

Wendy laughed, remembering the scene in Burke's bedroom last week after the storm. That had been far from innocent in her eyes, even though technically she supposed it was. Certainly what had passed between them made her feel irrevocably committed.

At five o'clock, David still hadn't shown up. Meg and Wendy left the office together. They peered up and down the corridor, scanning it thoroughly, but there was no sign of him.

'It looks as though you might be safe after all,' Meg said. 'Maybe he's given up and gone home. Ken and I are going out to dinner tonight. I'll ask him if David has checked out.'

'Thanks, Meg. I think he probably has, but it would make me feel better about it to know for sure.'

They said goodnight then, and Wendy went for a short swim at the little cove where she and Burke had gone on his last night. She had it all to herself now, and as she floated lazily in the water, remembering how he had held her, called to her, she gradually began to forget about David.

After half an hour, she got out of the water, put on her white terrycloth robe, and started walking slowly back up the path to the hotel to shower and change for dinner. She kept thinking to herself, tomorrow night Burke would be back.

Her heart leapt with a thrilling, piercing stab of desire at the thought of seeing him again, of being once again in his arms. Would he still want her? What had he been thinking during the past week he had been away?

Wendy went into her room and locked the door behind her. She took off her wet swimsuit and got under a warm shower.

She soaped and rinsed herself, then, as she was getting dried, she heard a knock on the door. She grabbed her robe off the hook on the back of the bathroom door and slipped it on. It was new, a silky Japanese-style kimono that tied in the front. She went to the front door.

'Who is it?' she called.

'It's me. David,' came the answer.

Her heart sank. Oh, no, she groaned to herself. Just when I thought I'd got rid of him for good. Quickly, she tried to collect her thoughts. I must be firm, she decided.

'Go away, David,' she said in a hard voice. 'I don't want to see you. Go back to Baltimore, back to your wife. Try to work things out with her.'

'I don't want to work things out with her,' he said, his voice rising. 'I want you.'

'David, be quiet,' she said. 'You'll create a scene. Now, please leave.'

There was silence for a while on the other side, then he began banging on the door. Wendy jumped, alarmed.

'I don't care if I do create a scene,' he shouted. 'I've got to talk to you. Let me in.'

'David, for God's sake, be quiet,' she pleaded.

'I'll be quiet—I'll even leave—if you'll just talk to me. Ten minutes is all I ask. Then, if you want me to, I'll leave,' he promised.

Wendy's thoughts raced. Did he mean it? Should she take a chance and trust him? Ten minutes, he said, then he'd go. He began to pound on the door again. She felt trapped. If she didn't let him in, he was capable of standing out there banging all night. If she let him in for ten minutes, he might keep his promise and go.

She decided to take the chance. She got her key out of her bag and turned it in the lock. She drew her robe closely about her and opened the door.

'All right, David,' she said coldly, stepping aside so that he could come in. 'Ten minutes.'

Eagerly, he crossed the threshold and shut the

door behind him. He stared at her, his eyes travelling up and down her body. Wendy began to wish she had dressed before she let him in—the thin silk of the robe revealed more than was safe. She crossed her arms in front of her and glared at him.

'You've changed, Wendy,' he said, taking a step towards her. His bright blue eyes were gleaming. 'You seem older, more mature and infinitely more desirable.'

She turned and walked away from him. 'If that's true,' she said, 'it's because you taught me such a bitter lesson.' When she was across the room from him, at a safe distance, she turned around. 'Now, what did you want to talk to me about? You haven't much time left.'

'Oh, Wendy,' he began. 'Can't we start all over again? I know I was wrong, terribly wrong, but I'll make it up to you. Won't you let me even try? Can't you forgive me?'

'David,' she said more gently, 'I do forgive you. But can't you see it's over? It should never have begun. It was based on a deception, of me and of your wife. What about her? She has some rights, too. Don't you see?'

He gave her a sulky look. 'I told you,' he said. 'That's over.' He thought for a moment, then his face brightened. 'I'll tell you what. I'll leave—now, tonight, if I can—go back to Baltimore, then when the divorce is final, I'll come back. We can start all over again.'

'No, David,' she said firmly. 'It's over.'

The sulky look deepened into anger as her words finally seemed to sink in. He gave her a malevolent look out of eyes narrowed to slits.

'There's someone else, isn't there?' he said thickly.

She raised her chin and clutched the robe more tightly about her. She knew his pride was hurt, but she was through with lies and evasions.

'Yes,' she said simply. 'There is.'

The blue eyes flashed fire, and in three long strides he had crossed the room and clutched her by the shoulders before she could move.

'No,' he exclaimed, his eyes boring into her, 'you belong to me.'

She twisted under his grasp. 'Let me go, David. You're hurting me.'

For reply, he bent his head and clamped his mouth viciously on hers. She writhed under his unwelcome touch, but he only held her more closely to him.

Her head whirled, and panic rose within her. She beat on his chest with her fists, but this only seemed to enrage him. He began pushing her towards the open door of the bedroom, his mouth still firmly on hers. She continued to struggle, and through the jumble of confusion in her head, she heard a small end table tip over, the lamp on it crashing to the floor. To her horror she felt one of his hands sliding under the loosened robe, slipping it off her shoulder . . .

By now he was like a madman, and Wendy tried vainly to collect her thoughts. The more she fought him the more he became inflamed, so with an enormous effort of will, she made her mind calm and her body relax.

Gradually his hold on her slackened as he felt her struggles subside. She thought if she could just get away from him long enough she might be able to run into the bathroom and lock the door.

By now, her robe was half off one shoulder, gaping open at the front. She saw him look down and, with a groan, drop one hand, the other still firmly grasping her around the waist. When she felt his hand on her breast slowly parting the robe further to expose the white flesh beneath, she closed her eyes tight and gritted her teeth, hardly able to suppress a scream of revulsion.

If she could just calm him, she kept telling herself, she might be able to get away.

Then, suddenly, through the pounding in her head and the ringing in her ears, she heard a sound from the other room. Meg, she thought, her hopes rising.

'Wendy,' a voice called. 'Are you all right? I knocked, but . . .'

She raised her eyes in horror. There, standing in the doorway, taking in the whole incriminating scene, stood Burke Flint. Wendy realised immediately how it must look to him. As she watched, stunned, the look of concern on his face turned into disgust. His glance flicked to David, who had suddenly let her go at the sound of Burke's voice. Wendy pulled the edges of the robe together, covering herself.

'Oh, Burke,' she cried. She ran to his side and clung to his arm. He looked down at her with utter contempt in his eyes.

'Sorry to barge in on you like this,' he said in a cold voice, 'but when I saw the overturned lamp, I thought something might be wrong. Obviously, I was mistaken.'

Wendy felt as though a large bucket of iced water had been thrown over her. She released him, tied her robe more securely together and gave him an entreating look.

'You weren't mistaken, Burke,' she said in a rush. 'David forced his way in here . . . well, not exactly forced . . . I mean, I told him he could stay for ten minutes, just to explain . . .'

'And who is David?' Burke asked in a cool tone. 'Obviously an old acquaintance, since John Frazier is your latest conquest.'

'I told you about David,' Wendy said, desperate now to make him understand. The cold remote look on his face terrified her. 'Remember? The day of the storm.'

Burke gave a harsh bitter laugh. 'Oh, yes, I do recall. The married man you had an affair with. I thought you invented the story, that you were only trying to impress me with your sophistication.'

'It wasn't an affair,' she wailed.

'No?' Burke asked. 'You appeared to be on quite intimate terms just now. Too bad I came home a day early. You might have got away with it.' He laughed again, but Wendy could see the masked fury in those piercing grey eyes as he gazed down at her with contempt. 'Well, you've made a proper fool of me, Wendy. I was even going to ask you to marry me. Enjoy your triumph.'

He turned on his heel then, and stalked out. She ran after him, but the front door had slammed behind him before she got there.

'Burke,' she cried, and crumpled in a heap on the floor, dissolved in tears of misery and humiliation.

She felt herself being picked up and carried into

the bedroom and laid down on the bed. Once there, she turned over on to her stomach, sobbing. Dimly, she heard David's voice.

'I'm sorry, Wendy,' was all he said.

At some point during the night, exhausted with crying, Wendy crawled under the covers and fell into a fitful sleep. She awoke at dawn's first light, and immediately the horrors of the night before assailed her.

She lay, wide-eyed, staring at the ceiling, the tears slowly streaming out of her eyes, down her face and on to her pillow. She felt as though her life had ended. She couldn't think. It was all she could do to support the dull aching misery without screaming.

She slept again, and when she awoke, she glanced at the clock on the bedside table and saw it was after nine o'clock. She raised herself up wearily and reached for the phone to call the office.

'It's Wendy,' she said, when Meg answered. 'I can't come in to work today.'

'Are you sick?' Meg asked, alarmed at the sound of her voice. 'Can I do anything?'

'No,' Wendy replied dully, 'it'll pass. Will you be okay with the work?'

'Sure. No problem. Get some sleep, and I'll stop by on my lunch hour to see how you are.'

'No,' Wendy said quickly. She couldn't face anyone, not even Meg. 'I might be contagious. I'll be all right.'

'Well, if you're sure,' Meg said dubiously. 'By the way, Ken tells me that lover-boy David left early this morning. That should be a relief.'

'Yes,' Wendy said listlessly. 'That's good.'

'Well, call if you need anything.'

Wendy hung up the phone and lay back down again on the bed. She hadn't eaten dinner last night, and her stomach cramped painfully. But the thought of food only nauseated her. She closed her eyes and tried to think.

The one thing that seemed certain was that she had lost Burke Flint forever. Every time she pictured in her mind that look of cold contempt on his face when he saw her, half naked, in David's arms, she wanted to die of shame.

She couldn't blame him, she thought. She could clearly envision what had gone through his mind. He had missed her while he was gone. Missed her enough to decide he wanted to marry her. Then, when he came back, a day early, he had come straight to her room.

There, he had seen the signs of a struggle, the overturned lamp. He had been worried about her. Then, when he had seen her with David, he had assumed the worst.

Wendy wished now that she had continued to struggle against David, to scream, instead of trying to calm him so that she could get away. Even if he had ended by raping her, hurting her physically, it would have been far better than losing Burke.

She slept off and on during the day and by late afternoon decided that she would have to get up and at least go through the motions of living.

After she showered and dressed, she realised that much of her feeling of weakness and lethargy came from sheer hunger. She went down to the coffee shop and ordered a sandwich and a glass of milk to take back to her room.

As soon as she had eaten she began to feel better, to think straighter, and she knew now what she had to do. She would have to leave this place, go back to Baltimore, and somehow try to make a life for herself without Burke Flint.

There was a knock on the door. Burke? Her heart leapt, as she jumped up to open it. It was Meg.

'How are you?' she asked.

'I'm okay. Come in.'

'You may feel okay,' Meg said as she settled herself in an armchair, 'but if you'll pardon the expression, you look like hell.'

Wendy shut the door and sat down opposite Meg. 'I know,' she said. She had seen her face in the mirror, puffy with crying and ravaged by the emotional upheaval.

'Do you think you have the flu?' Meg asked. 'What are your symptoms?'

Wendy smiled weakly. It was past the time of hedging around with Meg. It wasn't a game, and Meg was her friend.

'No,' she said, 'it's not flu.' She laughed. 'I guess you could call it a broken heart, but I doubt if I'll die of it. Remember the old saying, "Men have died and worms have eaten them, but not for love."'

Meg thought that over for a moment as she gazed at her friend. 'Yes,' she said softly, 'but that's men, not women. Now, what's happened?'

Then the whole story began to pour out of Wendy, interspersed by gropings for tissues and tears, but eventually she got to the end of it and felt better for having shared it.

'So you see,' she ended up, blowing her nose and wiping her eyes, 'I've got to leave.'

Meg stood up and paced the room for a few moments, then came and stood before Wendy.

'I see,' she said in a curiously flat voice. 'Sure. You're going to run away again.'

Wendy gasped. She felt as though Meg had struck her. 'Meg!' she exclaimed. 'That's unkind— and unfair.'

Meg sat down opposite her again, leaning forward eagerly. 'Listen,' she said, 'you're in love with Burke Flint. He's obviously in love with you.'

'He hates me,' Wendy said miserably.

'Sure he hates you,' Meg said scornfully. 'That's why he came back a day early. That's why he was going to ask you to marry him. And that's why he turned on you when he saw you with David.'

'All right, all right,' Wendy said. 'But what can I do? He won't even talk to me. If you had seen the look on his face!' Wendy shuddered and covered her burning cheeks with her hands.

'You go down to his cottage and you *make* him listen to you,' Meg said firmly. Then her eyes and voice softened. 'You've at least got to try, Wendy. Listen to your heart. If you love him, if he's what you want, he's worth fighting for.'

'Oh, Meg, I don't know. I'll have to think about it.' She smiled. 'Thanks for listening, anyway.'

It was after dark when Wendy finally decided she couldn't leave Nassau without making one last attempt to talk to Burke, to explain calmly and rationally what had happened.

Ever since Meg had left, she had sat in her room

pondering, weighing pros and cons, getting nowhere except into further confusion. Listen to your
heart, Meg had said.

'All right,' Wendy had said aloud to the empty
room. 'I'll just do that.' And she got up, washed her
face and combed her hair and set out.

Now, however, approaching the cottage, she began to have second thoughts. What if he just shuts
the door in my face? What if he isn't even there?

By now she was at the door. Summoning up all
her courage, she knocked. She heard footsteps,
then, and the door opened. He was standing in the
doorway, tall and forbidding, the light from the
room behind him silhouetting his frame.

'I—I'm going to leave Nassau,' she blurted out.
'Before I go I'd like to talk to you.'

His face hardened, and a sneer began to form on
his face as he opened his thin mouth to speak. Then
he smiled sardonically, opened the door wider and
stepped aside.

'Come in,' he said coldly, politely, with a sweep
of one hand.

She walked past him into the familiar room,
dimly lit, and a chill pierced her heart at his hard,
distant manner. How could she even begin?

She stopped at the french doors to the patio and
stared out into the darkness. She heard the front
door shut, heard his footsteps coming towards her,
stopping. There was dead silence in the room.

'Well?' he said at last. 'Have you come to crow?'

She turned around to face him and caught her
breath at the overpowering longing for him that
seized her at the sight of his tousled black hair, the
curled lips mocking her, the grey eyes piercing into

her. He had a drink in his hand.

'No,' she said. 'I have nothing to crow about.'

Then, taking a deep breath, she began to explain. The words came haltingly at first—his steady silence unnerved her—and she faltered, stopped, then made herself go on.

She tried to calmly stick to simple facts, with no emotional overtones, no pleading, no tears.

'I had no feelings left for David whatsoever. When he showed up here, I was appalled. I did everything I could to convince him to leave, that I didn't care for him, that whatever had been between us ended the minute I found out he was married.'

Still Burke was silent. The only sound in the room was the clink of the ice in his glass when he raised it to drink from it. His eyes never left her face, and his expression was totally inscrutable. She lowered her eyes and waited, and finally he spoke.

'Why are you telling me all this?' Burke asked, his voice cold and remote.

She swallowed. Every vestige of pride was gone. She wanted to turn and run away from those hard, penetrating eyes, but every instinct told her to stay and see this through.

'I—I,' she stammered. 'Because I love you, that's why,' she blurted, on the verge of tears.

It seemed to her then, through misty eyes, that his face softened, but if so it was only for a moment. He stood up, put his hands in his trouser pockets, and cocked his head to one side. Then he slowly, deliberately, looked her up and down.

'That's very interesting,' he drawled. 'Would you care to prove it?'

'How?' she asked in a small voice.

'Take your clothes off, and I'll show you,' he said, grinning nastily.

Wendy gasped, her cheeks flaming. She half turned, as if to run. Then Meg's words came to her. 'If you really want something badly enough, you'll take risks to get it and won't count the cost.'

She felt suddenly calm. She gazed directly into those mocking grey eyes. Then, slowly, she raised her hands and began to unbutton her shift.

As she reached the last button and allowed the shift to slip off her shoulders with a little shake, she saw the fire leap into his eyes. She stood before him unafraid, then reached behind her back to unhook her bra.

She heard him give a low groan and in one second he had crossed the room and she was gathered into his strong arms.

'Oh, Wendy,' he breathed, 'my poor baby, what have I done to you?'

She clung to him with all her strength as he stroked her hair, her shoulders, her bare back. Then his lips found hers, and he kissed her as though he wanted to devour her.

'Oh, my God,' he breathed into her ear when he finally tore his lips from her. 'I thought I'd lost you.'

She clasped him tightly around the neck, standing on tiptoe to run her hands over his shoulders and up into his thick black hair.

'Never, Burke,' she whispered, 'never.'

He put his hands on her shoulders and held her away from him, peering down into her eyes.

'I love you, Wendy,' he said with deep emotion,

a tremor in his voice. 'I want to marry you. Say you will.'

She smiled up at him, her face glowing with love, and reached up to take one of his hands in hers. Slowly, she guided it down and placed it over her breast. 'Of course I'll marry you, Burke,' she said. 'Any time, any place.'

The hand on her breast began gently kneading, slipping under the lacy half bra. Still he held her gaze in his.

'I want you, Wendy,' he said in a low, strained voice. Then he sighed and removed his hand, placing it again on her shoulder. 'But we're going to wait and do it properly.' His tone lightened. 'I always did want a virgin bride.' He reached down and picked up the discarded shift, helped her into it, and slowly buttoned it up the front.

There was only one factor that marred Wendy's perfect happiness. She had to be sure he trusted her. She looked into his eyes.

'Do you believe me, then, Burke?' she asked. 'About David?'

He touched her nose lightly with his forefinger. 'You believed me about Andrea, didn't you?' he asked. 'That there was nothing between us even though she stayed here at the cottage with me.'

'Well, yes, of course I did,' she replied.

'Then give me a little credit for trust, too,' he said. 'It cost me just as much to tell you the truth about Andrea as it cost you to tell me the truth about David.'

'I don't understand,' Wendy said, puzzled.

'I wanted you to think Andrea and I were having an affair,' he explained. 'I was attracted to you from that first magical moment on the beach when I thought you were a mermaid. Everything I did after that was a feeble, futile attempt to get you out of my system. I thought if you believed I was involved with another woman, I'd be safe. I didn't want to fall in love.' He sighed. 'But that afternoon of the storm I had to tell you the truth and I knew I was lost.'

Silently, Wendy thought that over. Then she said, 'I tried to stay away from you. If you were afraid of falling in love with me, why did you keep after me?'

He ran a hand through his hair. 'I have my weaknesses, too, you know. Damn it, I *couldn't* stay away. And your obvious desire to keep out of my clutches only whetted my appetite for you.'

'I would have had an affair with you, you know,' she said quietly.

He gave her a tender look. 'I know. But by then I knew I was in love with you, and love doesn't take advantage of the loved one's weakness.' He grinned. 'Besides, I told you. I wanted a virgin bride.'

She gave him a quizzical look and reached out and ran her hands up under his shirt, over his chest.

'You may not get your wish,' she said provocatively as her fingers trailed lightly over the quivering muscles.

His eyes widened. 'Why, you little . . .'

She laughed. 'Tell me something, Burke. Did you decide you wanted to marry me before or after you found me with David?'

He stiffened, then grinned. 'That's something you'll never know, little Wendy,' he said, and gathered her up into his arms.